D0169522

Acknowledgements

Portions of this book have appeared in slightly different forms in:

Mirage (ed. by Kevin Killian and Dodie Bellamy)
Nobodaddies (ed. Doug Rice)
Tasting Life Twice (ed. by E. J. Levy, AVON Books)
Hers (ed. by Terry Wolverton and Robert Drake,
                    Faber and Faber)

Thanks to Phil West for reading.
Thanks again to Chris for everything.

A MODERN BESTIARY

THE DOGS

REBECCA BROWN

City Lights Books
San Francisco

Cover design and text illustrations by DiJiT
Book design by Robert Sharrard
Typography by Harvest Graphics

Library of Congress Cataloging-in-Publication Data

Brown, Rebecca, 1956–
    The dogs : a modern bestiary / by Rebecca Brown
       p.   cm.
    ISBN 0-87286-344-1
    1. Dogs—Fiction. I. Title.
PS3552.R6973D64   1998
813'.54—dc21   98-36228
                                       CIP

City Lights Books are available to bookstores through our primary
distributor: Subterranean Company, P. O. Box 160, 265 S. 5th St.,
Monroe, OR 97456. Tel: (541)-847-5274. Toll-free orders
(800)-274-7826. Fax: (541)-847-6018. Our books are also available
through library jobbers and regional distributors. For personal orders
and catalogs, please write to City Lights Books, 261 Columbus
Avenue, San Francisco, CA 94133, or visit us on the World Wide
Web at: www.citylights.com.

CITY LIGHTS BOOKS are edited by Lawrence Ferlinghetti and
Nancy J. Peters and published at the City Lights Bookstore,
261 Columbus Avenue, San Francisco, CA 94133

for Barbara Ann Wildman Brown

And lo, Thou wert close on the heels of those fleeing Thee, God of vengeance and fountain of mercies, both at the same time, who turnest us to Thyself by most wonderful means.

—St. Augustine
Confessions

I fled Him down the nights and down the days;
I fled Him down the arches of the years;
I fled Him down the labyrinthine ways
Of my own mind. . .
I hid from Him.

—Francis Thompson
"The Hound of Heaven"

THE DOGS
a modern bestiary

DOG...IN WHICH IS ILLUSTRATED IMMANENCE

One night I saw a dog in my apartment.

It was a big dog, tall and black and lean, with pointy ears and long taut slender legs. It had black eyes and auburn tips on its face and feet and it didn't move at all. I was afraid and held my breath and the dog did too. Then after a while its muzzle twitched and I could see its teeth. It growled low in its throat and I was terrified. Then the dog stopped twitching and its mouth closed but it was like there was an x-ray and I could see through the skin to its teeth. I could see the tension in its mouth and how the dog was trying to keep from snapping.

I held my breath as long as I could. When I let it out the dog breathed too.

Nice dog, I said as calmly as I could, Niiiice doggie.

The dog breathed out slowly, indignantly, like I had not shown right respect for my superior.

I wanted to get away from it, but I was afraid I'd set it off. The closest place to get away was the bathroom. I slowly lifted my right foot and put it behind me. The dog watched every inch of me. I moved my left foot back a baby step but I was afraid to turn my back to the dog so I stepped sideways very slowly into the bathroom. When I got inside I locked the door behind me, leaned against it, shivered.

I closed my eyes and touched my fingertips to my temples, especially my right temple, which felt like something was pressing it, some hard metal thing like a wedge or a point. It made my right eye squint. I touched my fingers to my temple as if I could press it out.

I splashed water on my face and drank a huge glass of water. As I was drying my face I saw it in the mirror. I didn't look great, but at least I didn't see a dog. I decided to take a shower. I took off my clothes and saw my body.

The head was slightly bent aside. The hair was limp and hung in clumps and stuck out from the top. The face was white, the eyes were dark, the rims around them red, the hollows black. The nose was slightly swollen. The lips were pale, thin and cracked, the upper lip particularly. The neck was thin and had a blue-green vein that beat like an invitation. The shoulders stooped. The ribs and hips stuck out. The stomach hollowed in. The tits sagged. The skin of the torso, particularly of stomach and thighs, was the color and looked the texture of overcooked pasta. The skin of the arms and hands was slightly darker. The hands were veiny, thin, too big to fit the rest. The knuckles stuck out. The fingernails were chewed to the quick, the skin around them raw. The legs and arms were skinny and white and the knees and elbows poked out from them like fungus from a tree. The feet were pale though red with bunions and yellowish with callouses.

There was a patch of hair in the middle of the lowest part of the torso. A blue vein beat above it on the left, that is the mirror's left, my right, side.

I stood in the shower a long time. I felt a little better when I finished. I dried off, grabbed my peejays from the hook on the bathroom door and put them on.

My apartment is tiny, really tiny, only the main room with my bed and desk and chair, the bathroom and a little kitchenette. The overhead light switch is between the bathroom door and the entry door. I shut it off as I stumbled to the bed. The only light was the pale orange blur from the street lamps through the window.

I got into bed like I do every night. I rolled over on my side and pulled the blankets up to my face leaving only enough room to breathe. I pulled my knees toward my chest and my feet toward my butt. I tucked my head and pressed my fists into my eye sockets. It's the way I always have since I was young.

I was starting to fall asleep when I heard a click. Then there was another click. Then padding across the floor. One way, then still, then back the other way. Then toward the bed. I was scared. I could feel my body thinking "no." There were the clicks and pads then a few taut seconds of nothing then the leap. I felt the weight as it hit the bed. It moved toward the foot of the bed. It circled around in a circle, then two, then three, then pawed at the blanket and mumbled something and lay down.

I pretended that I was asleep. I lay very still and quiet and tried to breathe as deep as anything. After a while I thought I heard it breathing deeply. When the breathing had gone on like that and I'd convinced myself it was asleep, I pushed my cover down the tiniest bit and lifted my head the tiniest bit and looked down over the lumps of me and at the foot of the bed, as if it belonged, as if the bed belonged to it, I saw the dog.

In the terrible light from the street outside I saw the outline of the body. The butt was to the footboard and the paws were straight in front. The head was up. I saw the shine of the open eyes: the dog was watching me.

I woke up underneath a heavy weight. My ribs were squashed and it was hard to breathe. I couldn't move. I could barely open my eyes but I saw it lying on me. I wanted to leave but didn't want to wake it. I wished I could shrink or float above, outside us both. I tried to move my right arm. I pressed it down in the mattress so I could move it over toward the edge of the bed. But it was there too, on my side. I flexed my fingers. I could feel stiff fur, the edge of a leg. I tried to move my arm again and I was slapped with a paw. The paw scratched like the splintered end of a two-by-four. I felt the tops of claws like nails against my skin.

Let me out, I could only whisper. Please.

No answer.

Please, I whispered again.

Nothing.

In its own sweet time, not because I'd begged, it shifted slightly and I could breathe enough to stay alive. Then it didn't move anymore.

I tried to not feel anything. Not the crush of my ribs beneath it. Not my arms and legs like sand. Not my neck pressed down so every time I tried to swallow I was choked.

Please, I rasped again.

Then I felt the tongue and mouth go over mine and I couldn't breathe at all. I thrashed and tried to suck the air. I really thought I'd really die, I thought I was blacking out. Then it moved and I gulped for air, I sucked it in. Then its body pulled away from mine. I felt the butt and torso lift and I heard it straighten and stretch. The dog smacked its lips and yawned like it was a lovely, delicious morning.

When I could again, I sat up and looked. The teeth were white, the tongue was red, the eyes and throat were black. It yawned a gravelly little growl that slipped up the scale to a contented yip. It sounded like a baby's chirp. In any other circumstance it might have sounded sweet.

The dog got out of bed. Its back feet jabbed me when it jumped but I didn't make a sound. I was pretending I was dead. I heard it walk into the kitchen and sniff around then come back by the bed. I lay as still as death but I couldn't fool it. It stood with its head near the head of the bed and barked. I flinched. It barked again, commanding me. I pushed down my cover and dropped my legs to the floor. When I moved my body felt like lead but I stood straight at its command. It sniffed my feet and nosed my peejays and lifted the bottoms of my peejays with its muzzle to inspect me. I stood at attention, my eyes ahead. I felt the wet nose through the flannel to my skin. When it was done, the dog stepped back, wiped its nose with a paw, wiped the paw on the floor then sat on its haunches and waited.

I didn't know what it wanted from me.

After a while, when it was clear I didn't understand, the dog shook its head and sighed like I was dumb then looked toward the kitchen so I went there. When we got there it looked at the tap and barked. I filled a bowl with water and put it on the floor. The dog examined it carefully. Then dipped the tongue, which was pink and wide, and drank.

I watched it drink.

The dog drank deeply, thirstily, as though it had come from faraway.

I watched the sleekness of the pulling throat, the wet

and tender pink of tongue, the stomach, pulsing, lined with tits.

And suddenly I saw the dog was beautiful.

And so the dog moved in with me. She lived inside my life.

And every day she woke with me, and every single night she filled my bed.

2

BODY...IN WHICH IS
ILLUSTRATED
CONSTANCY

Every day the dog was there.

When I got home from work the dog was waiting. When I put my key in the door to the street I'd hear her whining all the way downstairs. When I walked up the stairs I could hear her tail thumping. When I got on my

floor I could hear her scratching on the inside of my door.
I'd stand outside my door and hear her growl and I would
press myself against the door and feel her inside.

I'd go inside and she'd jump on me. She'd press herself against me with her claws and tease and scratch me.
She'd whine and fret and shiver until I wrestled her to the
bed and we would roll around. Then after we'd exhausted
ourselves, we'd settle down. I'd sit up on the bed and she'd
jump off and sit at my feet and look up at me adoringly
and I would tell her all about my day.

There was a way she cocked her head, or drooped her
ears and got that long, sad, pitiful, weepy look that makes
me think she understood.

I told her all about my day then all about my life.

I whispered to the dog.

I told her things I knew she would not understand.

I said them anyway.

And it was good that though I did not think the dog
would understand, it was enough.

To say what would be said, what would no more be
left unsaid, was, almost, then, enough.

I told my dog the secrets and she kept them.

I told her what I'd never told and wanted not to know.

Then what desired saying changed.

I held the dog and told the dog and longed for her to
tell me and I acted like she did.

I needed this with mouth and hands and tongue and
every part.

I held the dog and told the dog and though she did

not answer, neither she leave.

The dog abided me.

But I was curious: Why did she stay? Why had she come? Why had she chosen me?

I was, yes, I confess, a little flattered. My home was humble, a dump in fact, too cramped for even me. If it had been a body it would be like mine, too thin and spare and angular and empty.

My building doesn't have a yard. I'd picked the place with the strictest lease: no roommates, no sublets, no pets. So I was afraid to have her seen, afraid I'd get evicted.

But the dog did not complain about our secrecy.

In fact, she thrived on how we were, and only ever always were, alone, inside, together.

I got over my uneasiness. I put it somewhere else.

I learned to accept the things she did, the things she made me do. I learned to fit myself around her ways as though the ways were love.

I loved it when the dog would sleep. She looked as innocent as milk, unguarded, open. I loved that she could look like that, as if that's how she was. I loved the way she looked the way I felt.

Sometimes the dog made noises in her sleep. I'd wake and hear the noises, hers, that sounded like the things I felt although I did not say. Her eyes were closed, her skin would shake, her brow and lips would twitch. I didn't know what I should do, if I should wake the dog.

But when the dog was troubled I remained with her.

She'd shiver when I had to leave and the bed was cold without me. I'd tuck the cover around her close.

I loved her.

I loved the awful beauty of the dog.

I loved the sleekness of the flesh, and then the tenderness of skin. The softness of the belly and the whiteness of the teeth. The neck, the tongue.

I loved the firmness of the patience, and the waiting. The lightness of the touch, and then the wanting.

I loved the catch before the spring, and then the spring. The opening, the going in, the dark.

I loved the tautness of the thighs. The clasp. Release.

I loved the stillness and the sleep.

How she abided.

Then later times, beyond the first, when I didn't want to, when I wanted, needed to be alone, or not to be at all, the dog was also there, remaining when I didn't want.

She watched me and she muttered in her secret way I didn't understand, as though she meant to whisper, I am watching you, Watch out.

I was afraid to ask for what.

* * *

Then it became as if my house was hers and I the grateful guest.

For even when I looked away, I saw her. Never in time to get away, but just before she'd lunge. I'd see her coming at me and was terrified.

She disappeared me bit by bit.

Then even when I tried to leave, though that was always harder, I could not.

Every day the dog was there.

When I got home from work the dog was waiting. When I tried to stay away but couldn't she would meet me when I stumbled home. I'd hear her whining at the door. When I opened the door she'd leap on me and press me back. Her black stump tail and tongue would twitch, her open mouth would pant and she would back me to the wall and hold me there. I didn't tell her Down! or No! I didn't tell her Please. She knew what she was doing, what I felt. I was afraid to say something that would really set her off.

I also was afraid the dog would leave.

For as much as she oppressed me I required her.

3

HOME...IN WHICH IS
ILLUSTRATED
STEADFASTNESS

Doesn't she know I could get in trouble? I could get evicted. When I signed the lease, it said, specifically: no pets. That made sense. This place is really small. It all surrounds so close. When I lie on the floor with my toes to the bed I have to fold my hands beneath my head or I'll bump into the wall. If I stretch my left arm out, I touch the kitchen floor, and if I stretch my right arm out, my desk. I can put water on for coffee with only four steps from my bed. I can be at the john in seven steps, and into the tub in eight. I only asked for what I needed. I didn't ask for more.

Didn't she know there isn't room for her? That I don't have a thing that's left to give?

I was puzzled when the dog showed up but she was beautiful and strong and, sometimes, kind and I had been alone. I couldn't imagine how I deserved such a companion. I had little to offer her. My home was humble, a dump in fact, too cramped for even me. But I had read my Baucis and Philomon. I had heard the tales. I had let myself believe that sometimes even the least of them, the humblest, the lowest of the low, was given gifts. I thought, What if she's an angel? A princess in disguise? What if this was a test, a chance, a golden opportunity? Or, what if the poor pathetic bitch was simply as desperate as me?

Of course I took her in.

At first the company was nice. She seemed so grateful! I liked the way she ran up to greet me when I got home. I liked the way she hummed so eagerly when I unlocked the door. She'd wag her little stump tail and dance around and jump on me and sigh and yowl with happiness. I'd feel her press me sweetly with the pads of her little feet. I'd close my eyes and know what she desired.

One day, after she'd been here a while, I stopped, on a whim, at the deli to get her a bone. I don't eat meat, and haven't for years, but I shopped there for milk and eggs and cheese and company. Everyone who worked there said how fresh and carefree and lovely I was looking. I wanted to tell them about her, a bit. I felt shy and proud and beautiful, almost. Almost like them. Though later I was glad, when things became the way they did, I hadn't told.

The deli-guy gave me a bone, his best, an especially juicy one. I took it back home to her. He gave it, he said, as a congratulatory gift. He wrapped it like a package. The paper was beautiful. I remember walking home and feeling loved and beautiful. The dog was sweet when I brought it home. She pranced and sniffed demurely at the bag. I knew she knew what it contained. She knew I knew she did. But we were playing, happy, overjoyed with giving, getting, being with each other. She whined like a baby and then like a boy. She squatted on her haunches and looked adorable. It felt so good to do the perfect, right surprise.

I brought her more. Then other little treats. It was hardly any expense when you think of how happy it made her. It made me happy too. It made me feel spontaneous and waited for and wanted. That can't be bad to want.

She seemed so free and casual, so full of life in a way I liked, in a way I wanted to be like.

Of course, she didn't have a care in the world, just stayed at home all day and took it easy. So when I came home after being out, she was very eager to see me and to visit with me. I'd get her something to eat and then get something for myself. I'd fork my salad carefully while I watched her neat little manners. She was so tidy! She cleaned up after herself like a little princess! She'd lick her chops with her sharp pink tongue, then lick the floor til it shined. Then she'd curl around and lie at my feet and look up at me. I felt so good and cozy and familiar.

I don't remember when she stopped looking so cute and warm and fuzzy. Everything looked fuzzy then. Then, believe it or not, she started getting tired of me, resenting me. *Me!* Who had opened my humble apartment to her, who had let her eat my food and cook with my kitchen stuff and wear my clothes. Yes, she even wore my clothes! I'd come home from work exhausted and she'd have snuggled into my favorite, softest shirt, the one I was planning to change into. She'd just be waking from a nap—I was exhausted, *I* was the one who deserved a nap—and the shirt, *my* shirt, would smell of her and have her hair and god knows what else.

I must've done something wrong.

I'd want to be alone but I couldn't be. I'd sit and close my eyes and try to rest but I'd hear her pace and growl like she was threatening me. I had to listen to her natter on and on in words I never understood, although I nodded as if I did. My eyes would get heavy as sacks. I could hardly stay awake but I couldn't offend her. I'd wait until she had had enough. Then suddenly she'd kill the lights and haul me, unresisting, into bed.

Spontaneity became a chore, familiarity, invasion. I began to resent her expectation that I would lug home some damned, wet, dripping bone, as if I got a kick out of her flinging me up against the door and tearing the bag from my hands. As if I thought it was cute the way she mucked up the carpet—*my* carpet —with her appalling lack of table manners. As if I liked the sounds of her slurping and gnawing, the snap of the bone in her teeth.

I mean, why should I get her treats when I couldn't afford treats for myself? What did she ever do for me? Here I was, putting her up—remember, I hadn't invited her—and she was eating me out of house and home and making the place a mess and shedding and dripping and slobbering. Your home is your castle, right? If you don't have your place to yourself you don't have anything. But here she was and she just kept staying on and on and on.

I started spending more time out of the apartment.

I should have known what was happening. How did I let it go on so long? Why didn't I say, Hey bitch, this has gone too far. I don't know why you came to me, or what you want but I can't take this any more.

Why didn't I just tell the dog to leave?

Because every night when I came home—and each night it got later than the last, and every night more dizzy than the last—the dog was there, all warm and fuzzy and welcoming, in bed for me. She was always there in the middle of the night, holding my hand as I felt my way to the bathroom, and holding my head when I was sick, when I felt the press against my temple, when I puked, and keeping the blankets warm until I could stumble back to bed. She never growled about me kicking or sweating up the sheets or the shouts I made when I bolted awake from a nightmare. She remained, despite her constancy, my truest friend. She was my only comfort. She met my every single need that she had made in me.

4

BONE...IN WHICH IS
ILLUSTRATED
CHARITY

One day when I walked home from work there was a butcher's shop. I hadn't seen the place before, but I don't eat meat, so maybe I hadn't noticed it. I hadn't been in a place like that for years. Not since I was a child and went with Mother out to get a special cut of something when Father was coming home. I was led into the butcher's like something was pulling me. I walked up to the counter and looked down through the glass and my arm was lifted up and pointed and I said, like someone else was speaking through me, That one.

The butcher wrapped it in see-through paper then wrapped it again in white. He wound it around in a perfect swirl like a candy cane or a barber's pole. He taped it smooth with clean white tape so it was long and round and like a cast or a dismembered thing. The butcher's hands were smooth and white, the fingernails very trim and tidy. He looked more like a doctor than the thing he really was. He slipped the white stump in the bag and handed it to me.

I walked home quickly. The day was hot and I didn't want the thing to spoil. I carried the bag by the string handle. It knocked against my leg like the bag of treats I carried when I was a child at Halloween.

Outside my apartment door I shifted the bag to my other hand while I reached in my jeans for my keys. I felt the swing of the weight of the bone. I looked in the sack and it looked up at me like a mummy's fist, like something from my childhood aiming up at me.

I took a breath so deep I felt like every single cell of me filled up and emptied out at once.

I hid the bag behind my back and put the key in the lock. I opened the door. The bare bulb in the hallway threw a line of light onto the apartment floor. As I opened the door the line grew into a triangle. Inside the apex of the triangle, exactly where she knew she would be centered in the light, there was the dog.

She was as still and solemn as the Buddha. For a second I didn't see her breathe. Then the light seemed to pulse and I saw her stomach move. My eyes zoomed in on her belly like a scene from a movie. I actually felt a bit ridiculous. I stepped into the apartment, closed the door and switched on the overhead light and things looked normal. Sort of. I began to move the bag in front of me.

The dog sprang up against me. Her front paws knocked my collar bone. I lifted the bag above my head and she lunged toward it. She stretched her huge black neck, her huge black jaws. Her huge white teeth were snapping. Then her back feet slipped on the floor and she fell. She whined like a baby and then like a boy.

I was convinced and terrified she would do anything to me to get the bag but she didn't. When she got her balance back she leapt again, but didn't knock me down. I lowered the bag but she didn't grab. Instead she crouched and growled. She pressed her forepaws flat to the floor and shook her butt and whined. I realized with relief, aghast and thrilled, the dog was *playing*.

She sounded like she liked it, almost, but at least as much as she hated it. So I played with her too. I teased the dog to jump then raised the bag up high and shouted No! She leapt and whined and cowered. I saw the tautness of her legs and thighs, the smoothness of her belly.

She was beautiful.

I played with her like that a while, then after a while, in my own sweet time, I commanded, Sit!

She whined then was obedient and sat.

I looked her over several seconds then pronounced,

like any proper school marm with her pointing stick, Good girl.

The dog looked at me and shivered. She was wild with need.

How much do you want this, I purred, How much does Baby want the bone?

She barked.

I snatched the bag up high. Polite, I ordered. We don't shout when we're polite.

Her muzzle twitched. I could see her teeth.

How much does Baby want the bone, I sing-songed through my teeth.

Her muzzle twitched again. Then she opened her mouth and yipped a perfectly well-turned yip like someone begging.

Good girl, I said, Gooood girl.

I held the bag a few more precious seconds. The dog was shivering.

I tossed the bag. She caught the thing midair then didn't even try to act demure. She grabbed it with her teeth and shook it madly back and forth. She was frantic to tear the paper off, frantic to get the meat. She threw it to the floor and chomped. I saw white bits of paper fly and silver strings of spit then clots of red. I saw her stomach heaving and her gnashing teeth.

When she'd torn the bag and paper off she dragged the bone to the center of the room—onto the carpet, *my* carpet—and gnawed. The thing was huge and muscly. I could see where it was hacked. The dog held it hard between her paws and put her teeth in it.

Then suddenly, she stopped. She swallowed, licked her chops and caught her breath. Then, in a gesture I guessed meant Thank you, she pressed her nose to my ankle and licked my shoe. I felt her tongue along my foot. The spot was wet and very slightly pink.

You're welcome, I mumbled, as she grabbed the bone again.

But by then, of course, the dog was no longer listening.

5

HOOd...IN WHICH IS ILLUSTRATED LONGSUFFERING

She made me into what she took.

I didn't understand what we exchanged.

I thought if I could turn around, make charity from need, I could release.

I thought if I could tell.

I told myself.

I told myself that no one else has seen her so I must have made her up. If only I think differently.

I must. I will.

See. Here I go:

There's nothing to be frightened of.

Yes. Here I go.

I'm going to take myself out for lunch. A nice expensive, self-pampering celebratory girl's lunch out. What a treat! Think of all the places I can go! All the places I've always wanted to go! (But I've always been too self-conscious because I didn't know how to act and everyone could tell I was a bumpkin.) And I shouldn't because I don't deserve it because it's so extravagant and think of all the starving people.

But there are so many nice restaurants!! Where good friendly people with good manners go and enjoy good food!

If I could go to all of them, I could. But because I have to choose, I can't decide. Each one of them alone seems less appealing.

It's better this way. I shouldn't be greedy and decadent in the first place. Besides, it's the idea of a celebration that counts. In fact if I did go to one of those places, I'd feel guilty—because I would *be* guilty—about spending all that money on myself. Money I don't have in the first place!

So I'll take myself out for a picnic instead. I can get some nice cheese from the deli and a bottle of cider and some grapes, (unless I'm still supposed to not get grapes because the workers are suffering. I don't know. I'm so out of touch with anything any more. I'll get olives just to be on the safe side.) And a nice fresh baquette and some chocolates and —

But all that's so bad for me! White bread and salt and sugar and dairy. Not to mention it's selfish, horribly selfish, to want that for myself, to even think of it when I should be thinking of starving people in the world and homeless people and homebound people and invalids and sick people, cripples and differently-abled and crazies who would die, I don't mean literally, I mean who would die with happiness! With gratitude! Who would cry tears of joy! If they could have a picnic like that! I'm selfish to even think of a picnic. I'm awful.

Awful.

I'm not only that. That's minor by comparison. I'm actually worse. Much worse. If I was really honest with myself, which is hard to do because I'm basically dishonest, I try to look away from things because I don't want to think about them, but if I do, if I make myself be at least partly honest, though can anyone, really, ever be entirely honest, especially about something like this? I don't know. I know so little about anything. But if I were as honest as I think I could be, I would have to admit: I am not just thinking of any generic homebound person or any invalid or lunatic or whatever. I'm thinking of Grandma!! Whom I haven't been to see in much too long—not since the dog—but *the dog does not exist.* For no one else has seen her, etc. and even if she did that's just an excuse for not going to Grandma's!

Grandma's a mess. Her bod's a wreck, what's left of it. (They've lopped a good percent.) And what remains is outta control. She drools and shakes — *it* drools and shakes — and you never know when it'll shit or pee or puke and or cry and she can't get out of bed. Her poor old brain is a mess as well. (She sees and hears and shouts at things, and they seem terrible, terrible things.) We can't tell if she's here or there or somewhere else. Or lost or just in agony. If I had even a half a heart or any discipline at all, if I cared about anyone or anything else besides my stupid little dogs —

Grandma doesn't know anything about this dog business. God knows I would never tell her anything like that. All she knows is that I haven't come to see her! But I will. I will! I will take this lovely exotic, but healthy celebratory picnic to her!

I will visit Grandma and we'll have a nice long talk and do lots of catching up. We'll walk in the garden and look at all her lovely vegetables and herbs and flowers and the pond and she'll be looking strong and great and tell me how good it is to see me and she'll be fine and strong and lucid and coherent and continent and—

Who am I trying to kid?

Yet, I must try. I must not give up hope.

I pack milk and cookies and a couple of cans of Ensure, vanilla, the one flavor that, so far, she has been able to keep down, prunes, candied ginger for digestion, mineral water, vitamins, the canned fruit cocktail she's always been so fond of, chicken soup and orange jello with marshmallows.

Who knows. She could be a lucky winner. She could be the one in a zillion.

I wear my blue and white checked dress with a fresh white starched apron. I look as pure as a Kansas girl. (In fact we lived there once.) My hair is gold and my cheeks are pink and my hands are clean and my legs are clean and I'm wearing white anklets and my eyes are bright and blue and I'm as pretty as a picture—not *too* pretty, not asking-for-it-pretty, just nice pretty. Also, my glasses don't have that black electric tape on them from the last time they were, from behind me, from the back, knocked off my fucking face.

The sky outside is clear and bright and blue.

Well, not entirely.

There is one little tiny white but not ominous looking, though actually more gray than white, cloud. But it's far away in the distance. Though near enough that the sensible thing is for me to also wear my cape. I put it on.

It's my riding cape (red). (It's also got a hood.) I stick in my arms and pull it around and tell myself it will, it *will* protect me. I take a swallow, like medicine, and pull up the hood. Grandma always, always said, she bore it into me: *Cover your head.* (I rarely do; I wonder if I had would it have helped.)

You'll catch your death, my Grandma said. She knew whereof she spoke.

I pack Grandma's things in a basket and cover them with a cloth and sneak (I guess it's habit) out of my apartment. I skip down the hill to the town square. There's a nice breeze and everyone is smiling and when I smile back

at them no one snickers or shouts at me and I don't let
forth with a string of obscenities, babble incoherently or
lift my dress and pee on the street. We simply smile like
we are civilized.

I go to the gate in the wall of the town and it opens.
It's a drawbridge. It lowers by magic. That is, I look
around to see who's seen me here, who's letting me, who's
urging me escape. I can't see anyone. I only see the flags
that wave on the battlements, the tower in the corner. I
see the glint of sun on something up there. Is it the metal
headgear, the pointy Prussian helmets or the visors of the
guards? Will they protect me?

I put a timid tiptoe on the bridge. I look down at my
little white anklets, my sweet little black Mary Janes and
remark, as if to myself, but really out loud in case someone
else is listening, how clean they are, how clean I am, how
undeserving of anything untoward. Then I stand there a
second and hold my breath.

When nothing hits me from above, when no one
grabs me from behind or flings me to the ground and pries
me open or crushes my temple as if in a vice or has their
way with me, I slowly release my fearful breath and slowly,
slowly, walk.

I walk the entire length of the bridge.

So I depart.

My feet on the ground outside feel strange. I know
I've been outside before. I've been this very way. Though
I remember only pieces.

She lives in the depth of the dark of the woods but I
believe I know the way.

The path is straight where it leaves the town and the ground beneath is smooth. The sun is out and bright. Terrific, I tell myself with hope, a sign! Then I look down and see my shadow. It looks someone's walking on my body. The feet step on the legs and chest, the head. I look away.

I turn to look at the town behind. The wall is tall with turrets. Flags fly, the beautiful long thin pointy two-tongued flags I remember from beautiful story books. There is the tower in the corner with a pointy top and just beneath that top, in the dull brown, mustard colored stone, there is the long black slit of an opening where some innocent or wayard girl or some drooling hag is imprisoned. I hurry away as the drawbridge creaks closed behind me.

I remind myself that I am doing good, that I am not afraid, that I am girded covered dressed accommodated medicated and I am on a mission of charity. I walk into the woods. I try to whistle a happy tune, but catch myself because they say that calls them.

I swing the basket at my side as if I'm confident. (Like that scene in *The Sound of Music* after Julie Andrews leaves the convent and before she meets up with the Nazis). My walk is brisk. My head's erect but the forest is dark around me.

I clutch my basket tight against my body. I feel, through my flimsy hood, my riding cape the color of blood which can hardly be expected to protect me, the scratching of the reeds the basket's made of.

I pull the cape around me close and pull the hood down tight around my head.

So I can't hear the pad of feet, or see the hand, the

paw, that grabs me from behind. But I can feel the
strength, it's animal. It throws me to the ground. I feel the
dirt behind my head. My skull is scraped. My scalp is torn.
My cape, the hood, my dress are lifted up. I kick and try
to scream but there is something in my mouth, against my
temple, pressing, hard and cold, then something up me. I
try to yell, I gag —

No— no—

It's not supposed to be like this. We tried to prevent it.
We did everything. Well, what we could. We couldn't —

Tell it different. Make it so.

Take a deep breath. In. Out. In. Out. OK. Now try
again:

So.

I've got the basket. I'm in the woods on the way to
visit Grandma who is a really strong cool stable retired
grassroots politico who worked with Eugene McCarthy
way back when and was the first white woman in our
town to march for Civil Rights and was arrested for
protesting nukes and became a member of PFLAG and
stopped eating red meat way before anyone else did and is,
in short, just an amazing old gal who is enjoying her
retirement by working in her amazing garden.

(Much better.)

I'm going to visit her just to hang out. This is not a
charity call. The basket isn't a care package for her, it's just
my backpack for the weekend. Though of course, it does
include a little something by way of a house gift for her.
(She raised me right.)

I know the way to the house. I've been there.

A big burly woodsman comes up to me and says he'll walk with me because there might be wolves, but I am not afraid. My Grandma's lived here years and I haven't seen one.

He's just doing his job, I tell myself, warning people of every remote possibility so the woodsguys won't get sued. I mean, of course there could be wolves. There could be lions or tigers or bears or nuclear fallout or the E-coli virus. There could be dogs.

The woodsman, who has the most concerned, compassionate, deep dark eyes, offers to walk with me, to make sure I'm all right, but I tell him no thanks, I'm not afraid.

He really seems to want to go with me. Are you sure you'll be all right? There've been reports, he says, of rabbit hutches and chicken coops . . . of howling. He sounds protective yet respectful too.

But I'm a big brave girl and tell him firmly, No. He shrugs, tips his white hat, turns away, then turns back a final time. If you change your mind —

I say thanks again and wave him off.

The forest is getting darker and I hear the sounds of animals getting ready for bed, the chirrups of squirrels and chirpings of birds and babbling of brooks. It sounds as sweet, benign and orchestrated as a Disney soundtrack. I wouldn't be surprised to see some cartoon deer and bunnies peeking out from behind a friendly tree.

I swing my basket at my side and start to whistle a happy tune when I hear something. Another creature readying for bed?

I listen but hear nothing.

I walk on to Grandma's house.

The cottage is a rustic wooden A-frame. Knotted wood. There's a window on either side of the central front door. Smoke curling from the chimney. Honey-colored light through the curtained windows. Pink and white and blue flowers in a yard of soft green moss. I follow the stepping stone path to the door and knock.

The sound inside is not her voice.

Then suddenly it's dark, it's night, it's terrible again.

Again I knock.

The sound is growling.

I try the door. It's locked. I beat against it shouting, Grandma! Grandma! Grandma!

I hear a rip and the sound of a struggle.

I pull the concealed 45 I pack from my jacket. (That's something wrong; the dogs won't let me carry this. I don't know how I get to here.) If some goddamn animal has laid a single hand on her I'll kill it. I swear. I'll blast its fucking brains out. I'll press it to the temple, the right one, squeeze it hard the eye will squint and I will blast those fucking brains into next year.

I can't do any of that, of course. Not yet.

I shoot the lock and kick open the door.

The room is white and hot with light. I blink. In a couple of seconds I can see the big black pot in the fireplace over a fire that crackles with cozy warmth. I hear something simmer. It smells good, like fresh baked bread and Grandma's garden stew. The table is set for two, with her favorite dish and mine, and there's a pitcher of fresh white milk and a bowl of bright red apples. It looks the way it always looks, it always looked, except Grandma isn't sitting there.

She's in the bed. But not her bed. It's not the hand hewn wooden, fluffy feather bed she loves. It's a hospital bed. The metal glints like blades. It's not her handmade quilt that covers it, the one with patches the same as my clothes, it's hospital issue blue.

She's on her back on the metal bed and the straps have strapped her down and tight and an IV's pumping something in and a nose drip is sucking something out and another tube is up her nose and her skin is as white as a bottom fish.

Someone's behind her in hospital whites that could have been worn by Frankenstein or Kildare. The mouth and nose are covered but I recognize the eyes: the kindly woodsman.

He glances at me a second. His eyes are kind, resigned and deeply, deeply sad. The hope he has is the size of his hands. He looks down again, intently, at his surgery.

He puts his hands inside her head. He's pulling something out.

In an instant I'm behind him. I am close enough to smell his sweat and feel his body's heat as he leans over her.

Her eyes are closed. Her mouth is slack and skin is white, translucent.

It's just the green line on the screen that makes me know, I think, that she is still alive. Except she doesn't look like her. Her body is no more her own. She looks like she's away. I wonder if she's somewhere there is peace.

He tries to cut away what's killing her but can't.

It's gnawed inside. It's fastened tight. It holds her with its teeth. It has turned into her.

*   *   *

Who was the wolf in that old tale, who ate the old and tried to get the girl has grown, in this new telling, from within. It's what becomes her.

We don't know how it entered. Like an angel through the ear? A bull? A bolt of light? Was it conveyed in air? Or through another's blood? A bite? A thing that is passed down?

6

DΛRK...IN WHICH IS
ILLUSTRATED
COMPASSION

The girl is mewling. Weeping in her beer. She's crying over milk that's spilt. (There is no milk; was never milk to spill.) She's snuffling and blubbering. (Nor beer.) Her nose is wet. Her eyes are red. Her face is red and there are drool and snot across her face. The drool and snot are drying, dried, to brittle crusty patches at the edge of her. But where she's still producing, she is wet. Ridiculous tears. The lashes of her eyes are clumps. She's wet inside her ears, inside the collar of her shirt. Her skin is cracked and stinging and she smells the way one does.

She looks the miserable mess she is.

She looks that way to whom? To someone else, for one can't see oneself like this, or, not entirely. To someone else, then. Many.

So she is not alone, not far away; she's here. In front of us here gathered to observe.

She has been put the place she is, though whether by herself or them, or through the wisdom of Miss Dog, or by her own unlearned stupid self, as if she likes it here, as if she wants to be observed like this, humiliated, stupid, wet. She does not leave. No, as we still observe, she stays, unmoving, where she is.

She's on an empty stage, alone.

She sits on the floor, her knees drawn up, her head and neck and shoulders bowed. She's barefoot, in a ragged t-shirt, shorts. From where we are we cannot see her face.

Enter Miss Dog, upright on her stunning hind legs. She clacks in in her riding boots. The place lights up. She's wearing a tastefully tailored pair of breeches (the thighs pooch out around her); double breasted riding jacket; riding hat (her ears stick out of the top, toward the sides); black leather gloves. What else? Of course—the riding crop!

She hears the clack of her perfect heels. She tries hard to compose herself. She sniffles, wipes her nose with the heel of her hand,

*an upward movement along her nostril holes, then wipes the sleeve
of her tattered arm across her weepy face.*

Where on god's green earth did she get her atrocious manners?

She doesn't know. She sniffles again.

*Miss Dog sniffs, not a sniffle, but a superior snort. She looks
down her elegant nose at her, to secure her attention and ours.*

*She trembles tries to still herself. She chokes on her nervous
spit. Sniffles. Blubbers.*

Miss Dog: *(disdainfully)* What are you blubbering
about?

She: *(blubbering)* I—I'm not b- b- blubbering.

Ms. D: *(shrilly, with a hint of a German accent)* Do not
attempt to contradict! I repeat, What are you blubbering
about?!

She: I—I don't know.

Ms. D: *(mock sweetly)* She doesn't know. She doesn't
know. She isn't very smart, is she?

She: *(sniffling)* N—no Ma'am.

Ms. D: No indeed. Our poor dear little child is an
idiot, a worm brained moronic *(spits out)* Girl. *(Lifts her
nose upward. We see it twitch like she is trying to identify some
far away, exotic scent.)*

She: *(nodding her head in agreement, ashamed. Sputters.)*
Y-yes Ma'am.

Ms. D: *(shouting)* Do not attempt to interrupt! *(Clears
throat. Adjusts the lapels of her riding jacket and recommences)*
So our bit of a lady, our ugly wretched foul disgusting
bump on the wart of the hole of the ass of the universe
doesn't know why she's blubbering, does she?

She: *(Silent.)*

Ms. D: *(Flicks her riding crop against her palm once then holds it poised in the air above her palm, as if to strike again)* I said, 'Does she?'

(She's jaw trembles.)

Ms. D: *(Shouting)* You will answer!!

(She's body trembles. Mouth moves open and shut in a hapless attempt to speak. Gurgles inarticulately.)

Ms. D: *(ominously, as if each word is an insult)* Cat-got-your-tongue?

(She shakes her head no.)

Ms. D: *(Shouting)* You will answer!!

She: *(Finally chokes out a whisper)* C-could you repeat the c-c-c-question?

(Ms. D smacks the riding crop against her leather gloved palm.)

(She jumps in terror.)

Ms. D: *(Slowly, as if to 'reason' with an idiot.)* The question, to repeat, is: Does she?

She: *(cowering, whispers)* Does she what?

Ms. D: *(Jerks her pointy nose skyward and, like a hunger-maddened wolf, howls.)*

(She cowers lower, trembling.)

Ms. D: *(Goose steps around her in a circle, heels clacking. Whips riding crop against the thighs of her riding breeches.)*

(She's teeth chatter loudly.)

Ms. D: Silence!!! Miss Dog is thinking!

She: Oh. Sorry.

Ms. D: *(Spins on the toes of her riding boots. Glares, then as if to demonstrate what thinking looks like, points her nose up in the air again as if sniffing a faraway scent. Poises riding crop in one hand above the other palm. Then, exaggeratedly loud, to demonstrate what thinking sounds like)* Hmmmmm. *(pause)* Hmmmm-mmmmm. *(Growls beneath her breath guttural cur sounds, yips and snortles. Then also things that sound like pompous, academic, legal and/or psycho-babble words that cannot be clearly understood. Such as: transferred invert subtext referent object contextualizing marginalized tendencies inadequately recovered discourse.)*

(She's eyes widen.)

Ms. D: *Rapping her riding crop against her outstretched left forepaw:* Let's see if She can figure out *Why* She is *(mockingly)* b-b-b-blubbering.

(She blubbers.)

Ms. D: *(Slaps riding crop against her palm to punctuate. Enunciating clearly, with exaggerated calm)* Were you blind, deaf or paralyzed at birth?

She: *(Puzzled)* N- no . . .

Ms. D: Missing arms, legs, vital organs, facial features or digits?

She: No . . . but I —

Ms. D: *I* ask questions!

She: *(Nods weakly, then vigorously. Eager to show she's learned to not interrupt).*

Ms. D: *(In a voice Sherlock Holmes would use as he's revealing to the assembled dimwitted others the ingenious solution to the mystery he alone has understood.)* Then you were born complete?

She: *(Nods, though less vigorously, still puzzled.)*

Ms. D: And you were fed and clothed and cooed about? Bounced on knees, coddled, tickled, photographed by squealing, doting relatives?

She: Yes . . .

Ms. D: Then it is true that as an infant you were not bound hand and foot, hoisted up in the arms of a brutal uncle who smashed, by the holding of your poor baby feet, you, repeatedly, though always just short of what would have been a merciful, at that point, death, against the outside corner of your government-funded nightmare of an apartment building, or a majestic five-hundred-year-old cedar?

She: *(Squints stupidly. She wants to ask Ms. D to repeat the question, but doesn't dare to.)* Huh?

Ms. D: *(Very slowly)* Then — it — is — true — that — as — an — infant — you — were — *not* —

She: No.

Ms. D: *(Patiently, as if to a moron)* No you were not? Or no you were?

She: I — *(Puzzling.)* I was . . . *not* bound and smashed and . . . whatever you said, by my uncle. I don't have an uncle.

Ms. D: Then your answer is "yes."

(She shrugs.)

Ms. D: *(Sighing.)* Let's try something simpler: Is it not true that as a child you were *not* raped repeatedly and brutally, neither vaginally nor anally nor orally by human or other things, such as plastic toys, garage tools, medical instruments, home-grown fruits and vegetables and the like, thereby having the precious once-in-a-lifetime idyllic childhood you, anyone, deserves, denied you, by your brutal uncle, creepy grandfather, dear papa, an upstanding figure in the community no one could believe would harm a hair of your little head, or other monster or group of monsters such as a satanic cult, cadre of sicko UFO worshippers, or a repressed and entire Catholic and/or fundamentalist congregation?

She: I don't have an uncle!

Ms. D: *(Breathing loudly through her nose, to keep her temper in check)* Is-it-not-true-that-as-a-child-you-were-*not* . . .

She: *(Slowly nodding as she begins to get it. Then proudly as she does.)* Yes. It is true I was *not.*

Ms. D: *(Smugly)* I see . . . *(Smacks her riding crop against her palm again.)* And is it not also true that you were neither beaten, gouged, electrocuted, probed, burned by cigarettes or wood-burning-kit utensils, scalded, boiled, nor in any like way made to suffer, as a youngster?

She: *(Muttering as if trying to remember details.)* Hmmmm . . . not exactly . . . it wasn't actually a wood-burning *kit* . . . not a full bubbling boil . . . hmmmmm . . . . hmmmm . . . . *(hesitantly)* Yes . . . it is true I was not.

Ms. D: *(Cheery as a camp counselor)* Very Good! *(Then kindly, jocularly)* Now here's an easy one: Is it true that you were not locked into a 2 by 3 broom closet with nothing to eat but slivers of bread thin enough to slide under the door and water they poured on the floor you had to lick up and no clothing but the peejays you were wearing at the time of your sudden incarceration, which got filthy, for you were living in your own shit, and out of which you grew, without the benefit of light or fresh air or human contact for 10 of the first 12 yrs of your life?

She: *(oddly bold)* Surely no one could survive that —

Ms. D: We will do without your commentary, Girl.

(mock sweetly) But we would like an answer. Is it not true that you were not —

She: *(sighing)*. Yes, it is true I was not.

Ms. D: *(Slowly, raises the riding crop above her open, black-gloved palm, then abruptly smacks it down.)* And am I correct in stating further that you have been *neither* eviscerated *nor* disemboweled; neither amputated, nor added to (unwillingly, by means of silicone or other carcinogenic or unsightly or habit-forming substances); neither rudely compressed into the confines of a nail-lined box the girth and length of a small, child-sized coffin, nor torn asunder by raging buck stallions tied, by tight leather thongs, to your pathetic little arms, legs and — neck?

She: It is true.

Ms. D: *(nods sagely)* And it is also true, is it not, that you have *not* been diagnosed with an atrociously painful and progressive fatal disease that will slowly but surely waste away your ability to function, to walk, to speak, to feed yourself, to control how and when you shit, a disease that will slowly turn your skin to the consistency of an undercooked crepe, all holey and oozy and pasty looking, not to mention how it smells, and your bones to putty, and —

She: *(shouting)* It's true! I have not been so diagnosed, but —

Ms. D: *(not to be deterred)* But nothing!!! You have not been raped (whether at the hands, knives, guns and/or dicks of Serbs, Croats, Muslims, Bosnians, UN peacekeepers or anyone else in the former Yugoslavia), repeatedly then had to face the horror of surviving not only without the benefit of any medical, financial, social or psychological help, but also as the sole survivor of your beloved, irreplaceable and, needless to say, now very dead family?

She: Yes. I —

Ms. D: *(Raising her voice, for she is not to be interrupted)* You have *never* watched, helpless, bound, gagged and clawing, while your dear, precious angel of a nine year old was violated repeatedly in front of you by a gang of thugs!

She: *(Shaking her head as if she can't listen to any more.)* Yes. . .

Ms. D: *(Relentlessly, gleefully)* Nor have you been kicked out of your home penniless, friendless and recently blinded in an undocumented on-the-job injury! That your house, including all your poor possessions, has *not* been burnt to the ground, the victim of a suspicous arson! That you have *not* been marred, psychically and spiritually by, and fated forever to bear the mark of, your having accidently killed your beloved little brother in a hunting accident at the impressionable age of ten!

She: *(crying)* Yes! Yes! Yes! It is true I have neither borne nor suffered *any* of that!

Ms. D: *(Suddenly whispering, like the villian in a cheap melodrama)* Then what the hell do you have to blubber about.

(She clasps her hands over her eyes and hunches her shoulders in shame.)

(Ms. D glares. Slowly slaps riding crop against her paw, waiting for an answer.)

(She looks up at Ms. D imploringly.)

Ms. D: *(Fake matter-of-factly)* So what do you have to blubber about?

She: *(Whispers)* Nothing.

Ms. D: Correct! *(Goose-steps around She again, tapping riding crop.)* You will answer in a complete sentence. Again, What do you have to blubber about?

She: *(Mumbling)* I have nothing to blubber about.

Ms. D: Pardon me?

She: *(Louder)* I have nothing to blubber about.

Ms. D: *(Sing-song)* I can't hear you!

She: *(Shouting)* I have nothing to blubber about!

Ms. D: Again!

She: *(Trying to shout, but bursting into tears)* I have nothing to blubber about! Nothing!

Ms. D: *(Growling like a dog)* Tell me again, What?

She: *(Breaking down)* Nothing.

Ms. D: And what does that make you, Missy?

She: Nothing.

Ms. D: That's right, a whiny little self-pitiful zero: Nothing.

She: *(Mumbling like a bag lady)* Nothing . . . nothing . . . nothing . . .

Ms. D: When you think of all the things that *could* have happened, that *would* be worth blubbering about . . .

(She sinks down, blubbering.)

(Ms. D stands above her, glaring down, then chuckles. Ms. D squats down and puts her mouth very close to She and whispers) I can give you something to blubber about. Would you like that? *(Chuckles again. Stands. We hear her leather creak.)* Wait here. *(Winks)* I'll be back.

(Ms. D taps the riding crop against her palm and, whistling, exits.)

The trap door under the stage that She would like to open and swallow her whole remains closed. She stays unmoving on the stage.

Lights out.

She, blubbering, waits.

FIN

7

MIRACLE... IN WHICH IS ILLUSTRATED MUNIFICENCE

I t's like it happened to someone else. It's like it wasn't me.

I try to get away from her.

I go for a walk. I walk down Federal Ave, a quaint little tree-lined street that has somehow managed, despite the burgeoning commercial district a mere two streets away, to maintain an elegant, small-town charm. It's spring—late spring, early summer, some idyllic time of year—and the lovely trees are covered with sweet smelling blossoms, pink and white dogwoods, tender green shoots of something and tiny pink buds of something else—I actually know fuck-all about this kind of shit but I am trying, goddammit, to make this idyllic setting work. I have noted that it is sunny and that there is a touch of a breeze, in short, that it should be absolutely perfectly lovely.

Somewhere, close enough to hear, but far enough away so I don't have to see or talk to them, I hear the delightful shouts and cries and yips of little children. Every one of them, I'm sure, an angel.

Curiously, the street I'm on is absolutely quiet. There is no one else about.

Oh the sky is a lovely blue! Clear as a bell! Not a cloud for miles!

Well, maybe one . . .

The street is oddly empty and, when the children, wherever they are, suddenly stop, as quiet as a mouse with a sock gagged down its throat.

But I continue walking, working up to a stride. I haven't been outside for ages so my arms and legs are a little creaky. I breathe in a big, deep lungful of nice, fresh air. My arms swing vigorously at my sides. I tell myself it is indeed, it is *indeed*, a picture perfect morn!

I tell myself this firmly. Jaw set. Determined.

Determinedly, I breathe again.

Something catches in my throat. I try to cough it up.

It's stuck. I slap my chest and try to spit. It doesn't move. I hit my chest. It feels sharp. My mouth is dry. I try to swallow then my mouth is full of wet, except it doesn't taste like spit, it tastes metallic. I feel like I'm about to vomit. I slap my sternum, above my heart to dislodge it. My eyes water. I'm about to faint. I twist my hand above my shoulder to slap my back.

Then it *really* hurts. My belly's tight and something shoots. I feel I'm being kicked apart. I have never felt such fucking pain.

I'm sure that I'm about to die, except I can't. The thing stays where it is inside, though I can't tell exactly where or feel how big it is. There on the edge of busting death I teeter.

I'm too ashamed to knock on a door of one of these lovely homes—though there are side doors for the serving class—and I'm too embarrassed to just fall down and weep. Besides, along with the sweat that's suddenly sprung along my skin, I've been overwhelmed by a sudden urge to go home. If I am going to crawl into a corner and die, I want it to be my own little goddamn corner.

I'm sweating like a pig, my throat's as tight as a spinster's purse, my guts are a sausage about to bust, but somehow, I get myself home.

I open the door to my apartment and it smells horrible. Like blood and sweat and shit. The air is hot and steamy and there are mewling sounds. The drapes are drawn. It's dark. I fumble to turn on a light but there's a nasty growl. She sounds like she means it: Don't.

I don't.

I'm squinting with pain and squinting to see. At first I can barely make it out but then I horribly, awfully, do. Miss Dog is on the bed. She's lying twisted on her back. The sheets are bloody and black around her. Her belly's up, her legs are spread, and there in the hole between them, is a head. I try to blink the sight away but can't. Miss Dog is writhing. Her hips and the small of her back are taut. Her neck is twisted to the side and the veins are popping out. Her paws are clenched. There's sweat along her coat and skin. She's soaking. Her teeth are bared and gnashing and drool's dripping out and she's making horrible rumbling noises like the girl in *The Exorcist*. Her voice sounds like that too.

Help me, she hisses.

I get on the bed. I can smell even more. I've still got something in my throat and I feel even more like I'm going to puke. The head between her legs is wet and her tits are stretched with lines of pink where she is usually black.

She hisses again but her voice trapped. My throat is a bubble, a ball. My voice is trapped.

I move up the bed. My hands are moved between her legs then slip in her hole and my arms are up and in and my palms are sucked around the thing inside her.

There's a sucking noise and a pop and my hands are out and I hold up my bloody dripping hands and something is inside them. It squirms inside the sac. It pushes its feet and its nose for air. I pull the slime from around its muzzle, I slap its ass and it breathes.

Then Mama Bitch, née Miss Dog, who has been

holding her breath for the baby, roars. Her front paws swat, she can't speak yet, but shows me what to do. I lay the puppy next to her. The feet of the pup are small and sharp, the tail's a worm, the eyelids, seeds. It presses its mug to her tit and bites. She hisses again.

She hisses and there is another bulge inside the hole. It's like the circle on top of a cup then it grows bigger and pushes out. It's another head. My hands move up to take it. This one's easy. It pops right out. I catch it where it lands. I hold it up. My arms drip down. I slap it and it breathes and then I put it down beside her and there's another one. Another. Another. Another.

Between each one she howls and cries. Her body is wracked like she's deformed, like her insides are coming out. The pups keep coming.

There are more than she has tits for. I yank the ones who've fed from her — they yelp when I unhook their teeth — and shove the hungry in. I see their bodies claw for warmth. I pity them.

The last one wants to not be born. Already it's afraid of light, despises dry and air. It wants to stay inside, attached, unborn. It grabs the mother's guts and I grab it. It clutches hard. I start to rip. The mother howls, there's running blood, I tear it out: the runt.

She tries to crawl back in. I pull her out. Then she's unmoving in the sac, she's trying not to breathe. I poke the wet sac open, slap her ass. Her mouth, reluctant, opens, cries.

She cries aloud. Her skin begins to shrivel in the cold. I shove her to a tit. She turns and curls up in a ball. I grab her back and make her eat. When I uncurl I see her face. The mug is not a dog's: the mug is mine.

This scene goes on forever.

Then after forever it stops.

Then after it's stopped it's like it never was.

For who could bear a thing like that? But someone did. Someone who was not before was born.

I wake up and they're everywhere. All over my apartment. A litter. A dozen. Hundreds. They're all around, on top, beneath, against the tits and crawling. They are in the bloody sheets they've stained, beneath the windows, on the carpet, chairs. They're everywhere.

Radiant, as if transformed, Miss Dog rests in the midst of them, her precious ones, her flesh of flesh, her blood of very blood. She licks the bloody sacs from heads. She checks with mouth and lips and tongue that each of these, her lovely babes, her precious little miracles, is born complete and whole.

The puppies' mouths are greedy and she twitches when they bite. She flinches while they're draining her. When they have had their moment's fill and sleep, though not for long, she lifts her sweaty, weary head, and having borne the vessel's labor, radiantly smiles.

8

HOLE ...IN WHICH IS ILLUSTRATED JUSTICE

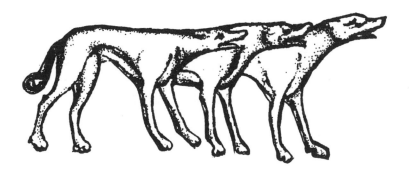

Something catches in my throat. I cough and slap my chest and spit. My mouth is wet then gushing, full, but it doesn't taste like spit, it tastes metallic. Then there's this incredible pain in my throat, like ripping apart, like I'm on fire then I hear this rumbling low inside me, then I'm sputtering and gagging and I see my mouth twisting. Somehow I see this like I'm looking down at me, like a close-up in a movie, though I'm also still inside me where it hurts like crazy.

Something is coming up out of me. There's a scrape like a rake and this thing prods up to the top of my throat. I shove in my fist to keep it down. I cram my hand, my whole arm in I push down my throat, into my stomach, my guts. I get my fist around it and hold it a second then can't, it's slippery, it shifts, big and moving, and my skin is stretched, my body, like a balloon, then I feel it tearing up through me and it heaves itself up and out like a concrete vomit projectile. I choke and gag. I cannot cry. My arm is shaking. My tongue, my ears and my nose are about to burst. My lips and cheeks have stretched apart and my skin is ripped. There's blood everywhere. The thing is bloody and black and slick: a paw.

I see this from inside myself like a movie where someone's knocking the camera around. But I also see it from above, like someone looking down. I see the top of my messy head. (My hair is a disaster!) I see a long black dripping stick sticking out of my mouth. Then I see my helpless hands reach up to grab it. I try to pull it out or push it back or break it apart or murder it. I can't. I also can't believe it except I have to because I'm not really above it, am I? No. I'm still inside myself, still me, and something, it, is tearing me apart and I feel every single stinking wrenching awful inch of it.

I loosen my poor weak hand from it, I'm giving in, there is no choice, then I feel another kick against my guts and my body heaves again and again there's something else pushing to get out of me. My insides push and my bloody broken throat and mouth are stretched again and there's another paw and then in a blurt another part and it kicks itself up and out and I pull and it squeezes out in a pool of muck. I fall on the bloody ground and gag.

Do I black out? Delirious? I must. For when I am aware again the pain of my guts is unbearable, although I bear it. So hard and sharp I can't feel anything else, although I do.

I'm lying on my back in blood. I feel a weight against me, warm. It's moving, breathing with my breath. I push it away from my body and see it tremble, newly cold. It whines, a sound so weak and pitiful I almost want to comfort it. I stop myself. I try to scoot away but hurt too much to move. It lifts its sticky, bloody head and opens its eyes for the very first time. I see it turn its head, its sniffing nose, to look for me. I watch her infant eyes adjust and see me.

The look she gives is strange to me, unclouded by the things to come.

My issue. My offspring. My flesh and blood. My baby.

She looks at me with, pure, adoring love.

I look away.

This from the hole, the holding place. The hidden, dirty, ugly place. The place from whence the waste, the nothing came.

MOTHER... IN WHICH IS ILLUSTRATED POVERTY

I'm poor, I'm poor, I can't afford to keep them, I can barely keep myself.

I live back once upon a time in a cottage in the woods. I live here all alone. No travellers ever come this way, no errant knights or pilgrims, ladies, saints. There's only me. I'm thin and dry and old.

The cupboard in my house is bare. Not even a crust, not even an empty cup.

I think I am about to end (please God) about to die. My bones are showing through my skin. My skin is thin as paper. I would like to die. I can neither clearly see nor turn my head, my temple, away. I am about to breathe my last.

When someone comes.

They snicker up and say they want their dinner. I try to tell them I have nothing but my mouth is dry and I can't speak. I scratch myself up off the floor and wrap my crooked fingers around my crooked, crooked cane. I shuffle to the cupboard and I open it and show the dogs it's bare.

I hear the click of claws. The young ones — Oh, they must be beautiful! — stand up on tiptoes to look. Their sighing, wiser elders don't. They know the way this goes from long ago.

I try to say I'm sorry and I wish I'd something left for them.

Sometimes I'm quick enough to turn. But other times I'm not and see them lunge. I always hear them rip my clothes. I always feel their teeth against then in my skin. I always feel them tearing out my heart.

I'm Old Mother Hubbard,
I go to the cupboard
To get the dogs a bone.
But when I get there
The cupboard is bare
So they have me.

10

CUP ...IN WHICH IS ILLUSTRATED TEMPERANCE

I try to leave for good but don't.

They let me out from time to time to keep the landlord at bay, to work, to bring them bones. I live for then. Sometimes I cheat. I go where they forbid. Where I consort with my own kind.

One night—it was a night like all the others had gotten to be, me stumbling home very late from my sleazy watering hole doing my very poor imitation of George M. Cohan with Parkinson's disease—the night took a turn for the even worse. It was even a little later than usual as I bumbled up the stairs to my apartment. I was doing my best to be quiet. I am nothing if not considerate of my neighbors. I tiptoed.

I prayed the dogs would be asleep. They weren't.

I opened the door of my apartment and saw the whole damned room was full of them. They had invited their relatives. There must have been a hundred of them, two. They were old and young and girl and boy and black and black with auburn tips. They had the stereo up full blast—the Cramps of all people! I slammed the door so their noise wouldn't wake the neighbors. The room was full of smoke. It smelled like booze. The carpet was crunchy with crushed-up peanuts and cigarette butts. Everyone was in their party finery. Their coats were shiny and smoky at once. I watched them dance like spirits, like wraithes. Some of them had this black and white and red make-up on their muzzles like ritual masks. I didn't know what they were readying for. Some of the little fuzzy ones, the pups, were nuzzling the tits of their adored, adoring mamas. Others of them were swinging from the ceiling— how did they get there? how did they stay there?—like bats. They were draped over my chair like feathers boas, like sultry girls. They were standing in the corners with cigarettes, like hoodlums. As soon as I was in the door a couple of them grabbed me. Their paws curled around me like smoke, but strong. I couldn't pull away. They lifted me and carried me through a cloud of that fake mist you see in stage plays, particularly in the more garish productions of *Macbeth*. The dogs had turned my bedroom, my humble abode, my dumpy little garret into a punk club on the heath. One of them put a cup into my trembling hand. I sucked it back, whatever it was, before I had time to worry or hope they had spiked it.

They pulled me around by my hands and nudged me in the back with their eager muzzles. They were not asking, they were telling me to dance. But I couldn't. I shook my head, which was a bad idea. Three of them scooped me up, sashayed me to the bed and lay me in it gingerly, as if I was their baby. One grabbed my cup to keep it from spilling. They propped me up against the headboard. I tried to keep upright while I watched them swish and turn on the ugly carpet. They looked like swaying, underwater plants. They were eerily, oddly beautiful.

But as every circus has its clown and every fête its wailing, warning penitent, so too this tawdry festival. And if I wouldn't dance for them, they would make do. They parted like the Red Sea did for Moses to let through, into the center of the crowded room, a particularly, peculiarly, spectacularly wretched looking dog. (Kudos to Make Up and Costume.) She was wearing one of my frayed and oversized, undercleaned, thrift store men's shirts and my spare pair of specs. (God knows where she found them! I thought they were lost!) The glasses were slipped down to the end of her muzzle and the yellowish, sweat-stained nose bridge pinched her moist black nostrils. She twitched to the opening they'd made for her and "danced." She jerked her head like a madwoman, crossed her eyes and lolled her head like a drunk. Then, in what sounded too embarrassingly familiar, she squealed in her best, worst, most screechingly awful human voice, Down! Down! Down! while she stumbled around as if she was completely, abso-fucking-lutely smashed. The rest of the dogs were chortling, then positively howling with amusement. I tried to be a good sport and laugh with them but the movement made me queasy. The most I could manage was a wan little smile. I felt bad about that: the bitch was talented! She deserved more credit for her really quite accurate, both in detail and in the broader execution, portrayal of her oft-unwilling, oftener unable, poor pathetic, hapless hostess, her miserable mistress: me.

But this was *my fucking apartment*, I moaned to myself, not theirs. I lived alone in order to, precisely to, avoid the embarrassment of having anyone — people, women, dogs, whomever — see me how I all too truly am.

For I had done my very best, my damned and awful only best, to keep my secrets to just me alone. I wanted no one else to know the dark hole of my heart, the pool of cess that bubbles in my brain. I didn't went a single soul to catch me in the act of being me.

But I couldn't hide myself when they moved in. They numbered every hair of me, each gasp of fear, each clutch of want, each shrug of hope that ever spasmed through me. They tapped my phone, my brain, my heart. I swear it's true, they monitor my dreams.

It's them that answer the phone these days. Whenever

I try to make a call, they sabatoge it. And the times when anyone else has called and I tried to pick up the phone, they beat me to it. It wasn't me who said those awful things, it was the dogs. They've kidnapped me here in my apartment, inside my crappy little life.

But I should only half complain.
The dogs are mean, all right, but are not wrong.

11

ANGEL...IN WHICH IS ILLUSTRATED PERSPICACITY

I f someone would come down to me.

If someone would come down and say.

If someone would come down and say in body, word or deed, then I would listen.

If she would say with mouth or tongue or word or

hand, I'd welcome her. I'd do the things she asked.

If she wrote me a letter I'd read it. If she sent me a story in Braille.

If she came from the sky, from God on high, in dreams or in disguise.

If she spoke in code I'd decipher it. If she gave me a book I would read.

If she told me to travel or bring her a fleece or answer a riddle, I would.

Even if she said it would be hard.

If she said, It's going to be like this, you silly bitch, I'm going to slap your stupid vapid face and beat your addled head and break your knees caps, tear your guts and kick you in the shin and tits and parts and hack the bloody heart from you and rip apart your limbs and yank your teeth out one by one, sans Novocaine, for even angels operate on budgets, gouge your eyeballs out and scrape off one ragged one by one your puny toe and fingernails and shove a prod, a hose, a bottle up your flabby ass and down and in each orifice and flail every inch of you then salt and roast what's clinging to the bones then crack those bones then drop the mess that's left of you from a forty story window into rush hour traffic in a major urban center that doesn't have any mass transit and watch as you turn into pizza topping and though whatever is left of you will be begging, pleading, crying for the end, for it to be over, it won't be. No. Because all of this you will survive, you little miracle. Yes, you will live to live with this, each day and every moment, every day and every single night of this, your wretched, too-long life.

For these are not the tortures of the damned, they are the daily trials of the living.

If someone told me any of that I would listen. I would do the things she asked. I would submit — oh happily! — with eagerness and gratitude if only — please — if she would tell me why.

I would do it all and joyfully. I would do it again and again.

If only someone, if only she, would tell me why then tell me it would end.

12

HOUND...IN WHICH IS ILLUSTRATED VIGILANCE

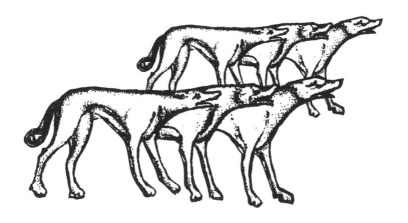

I used to think I knew enough about them.

For I had seen them chasing cars and running helpless cats up trees and pissing everywhere. I'd seen them frighten puzzled kids while fucking one another up the ass. I'd heard them knock the garbage over in the middle of the night and I had stepped on the piles of shit they left. I had discovered late, oh much too late, it always is too late, their crap that stuck to the lawnmower blades.

I'd seen them scratch and scatter fleas, and drool and sniff and rub and drag their filthy oozing butts across the carpet. I had seen them lose their puppy fat and grow their teeth and sic and bite till they drew blood. I thought I knew the worst of them.

But I was so naive.

Those things I saw, what all of us poor slobs can see, are not the things these special canines do. Those old, passé and boring things are just their leisure time activities, how they amuse themselves in their time off.

The dogs that I belong to, and I am not unique, I know of others (Grandma for one), the dogs that we belong to have a special job. They are the guards, the CIA, the keepers of the faith. They are Inquisitors. Their job is to observe and see, to catch one in the act. Then blame, remember and report. (Though I don't know to whom.)

They know about me what I don't. They know what I would not and they are merciless.

Sometimes the dogs get restless and I hear them growl from deep inside. I wonder if it sounds like this in Heaven.

I try to live in peace with them. I try to not be anything.

I live a siege inside with them. When I am foolish, desperate, when I try to think that I could get away and sneak they catch me.

They rub against the furniture and look at me. They pace beside the bed. They sound so close, like they're inside.

I wonder how long this is going to last. I wonder how long I can take it.

They lie with me and watch with one eye open. I know that in a heartbeat, in a half of one, they'd have me.

I try to live in peace with them and give them what they want. The dogs are hungry, ravenous.

The dogs sit on my face and eat my brains.

13

SERVANT... IN WHICH IS ILLUSTRATED HUMILITY

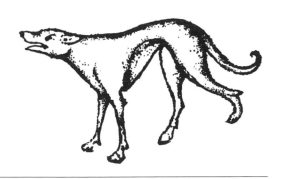

I'm brainless, stupid, air-headed. Dumb.

I never know as much as them. I never have the quick response, the witty repartee. But how can they expect me to? When I can't speak their tongue? Though sometimes when they're chatting, sitting up, their haunches crossed and holding their glasses adroitly in their forepaws, I can tell they're talking about important things. They're witty and urbane. They are extremely well connected. They drop the names of famous dogs they know personally on a first name basis, and when I don't look suitably impressed, they glare down their noses at me and snort dismissively. I don't know anyone. I am a dolt.

They let me know that nothing that I know has any value. They let me know it only is their tolerance that lets me stay around within their august presence. The problem they and any of the better sort of dogs are faced with nowadays, is the scarcity of reliable help. One simply can no longer find a decent girl. This forces them to keep my humble self as their domestic, hired help, their parlor maid, their girl. The dogs remind me often that without their kind benevolence I would be left out on the street, the lowest of the low, my kind, a harlot, moll, a whore.

Everything I do for them is wrong. Is not enough, is not correct. They tsk and tut and grumble at how inept I am. I know they doubt my honesty. (Can I be trusted with the silver? An afternoon alone with the little ones?) I wish I could remind them that the silver here is *mine*. (There is, in fact, that little silver cup Grandma sent me for my high school graduation). That the place where they reside is *mine*. It's *my* name on the lease. *I* pay the rent. *I* keep the fucking wolf from the fucking door.

They order me around. It only takes a look or nod, a tut or sniff, or growl, and I get at it. I say "Yessir" and "Ma'am" to brutes who, when they are on all fours, come up to the top of my thighs. Yet I cower, mumble, beg forgiveness for my poor existence. They hiss at me from feet below to stand up straight. Then when I do they slap me and tell me not to be impertinent. We know my place.

I listen, head toward the ground, while they demean, not only me, but all my wretched kind. I listen while they rant and bark. They yip about how soft I am. They snicker at my paucity of tits—a pair!—and how they sag and don't retreat when I'm not nursing. They prance like fops and make their voices squeak when they compare to my bloody, bitten finger nails their tough unbending claws. They pinch my flabby thighs and hips then flex their own firm muscles. They make me open wide then they guffaw at my stubby teeth, my begging mouth.

Then when they indicate they have had their fun, I curtsy, thank them for the lesson and I am dismissed.

Some of the time I don't want to die, but most of the time I do. I want to stick my face in the grinder and get it over with, but I worry who would help me flip the switch. Then who would clean me from the blades. For I've been taught to be considerate. Not make a mess. To clean up afterwards.

I mustn't leave a place like that.

The ones who most disparage me, who call me filthy, unclean, girl, are the very ones that sniff my ass when I get on my hands and knees to service them.

* * *

Officially, my duty is to teach the little ones. (The other stuff is on the side. But to whom can I complain?) I only teach the easy stuff, (they tell me I'm an idiot, not smart enough to teach more than a pup).

I teach the things our species have in common: to fight one's way to it then suck the tit. To claw to where one wants to get, to hiss when one does not. To growl to get a point across, to bite. To bare the teeth. To run in packs. To chase, to turn and fight. To bear, whelp and abandon.

I make a list: Post Office, Xerox, Groceries (with sub-heads): milk, bread, eggs, lettuce, TP, OJ. What else? I'm about to put my pencil to the paper again when one of them puts her teeth around my fingers and I let the pencil go. Another snatches the paper, crumbles my list and tosses it—two points!—into the trash. The dog hands the pencil and pad to another who prepares to take dictation.

Miss Dog clears her throat, stands abruptly, her perfectly trim ribs and perfectly flat stomach flexing like one lean muscle, and marches militarily to the middle of the kitchen. She clicks her tongue and nods at the cabinets. Two dogs leap onto the counter and open the cabinets. Miss Dog has placed herself in the exact center of the kitchen floor—it's like she's got a compass in her head she's so exact!—so she can see into all the cabinets. She does a quick perusal. The dog with the pencil hands it to the one with the paper. Miss Dog barks her orders. The secretary scribbles away furiously. Miss Dog's dictation is clipped, efficient. She's so much better organized than I am. Though I don't understand a word of their language, I can tell by the way it sounds that Miss Dog is spouting her list in alphabetical order.

When she finishes dictating the secretary brings the list up for approval. A mere glance and Miss Dog determines that it is correct. The scribe holds the list in her shiny teeth and brings it over to me. She wrinkles her nose as my distasteful hand approaches her to receive the note. My pale, hairless paw repulses her. I take the list and try to read. I don't recognize a mark. Is it Chinese? Or Arabic? Alsatian? Collie? Doberman? I *am* an idiot! I start to say, I don't understand —

But Miss Dog turns sharply on her heels and leaves the kitchen. I know she means, No whining!

I grab my wallet and head for the door.

As if she'd let me go alone.

Before I've got my hand on the door, a trio of the toughest, leanest, meanest ones are at my heels.

Outside it's a lovely day and people are on their bikes or walking or pushing their babies in prams. I try to walk slowly like I'm just out for a pleasant stroll. I want to say Hello! or Lovely day! or any of the precious little things that actually mean: I see you, fellow human. But every time someone approaches me the dogs leap up and paw my butt or nip at my thighs and I twitch away from them. They want me not to mingle with my kind.

About a block from the store I hiss at them, You're not allowed in the store!

They snicker.

OK, I snarl, Just try it. Suddenly I feel a shot of glee.

I know the people at the store. Well, I don't know them really, but I recognize them all and know their names from their name tags and they're nice to me. They say Hello! or Lovely Day! or ask me how I am. I tell myself they'll know how to take care of the dogs. I'm almost happy.

There's this one huge, muscular deli woman with a blood-splattered apron and white hairnet and tremendously powerful hands. I imagine her chasing the dogs from the store with a cleaver and I feel wonderful. I can't wait for her to meet them.

The dogs trot in behind me through the automatic door. I take a quick look around expecting, hoping, someone will notice them. The people who work here go out of their way to carry bags for shuffling old guys with canes, to walk new immigrants who don't know their way around a supermarket through the aisles, to listen to, then pat the hands of lonely old ladies and retarded people. I think of the nice nerdy day manager, the guy who pretends not to notice when I buy tampons but always says something nice like "how about a plastic bag for your frozen juices?" as if it's something he's thought of especially for me. Or maybe the big sweaty bakery man who has, more than once, told me I need to fatten up and stuck a donut—free of charge—into my bag of bread. Or the extremely cute girl who arranges the vegetables, and to whom, for obvious reasons, I have never said a word. I grab a cart and push it down the aisle.

The dogs are frisky, nipping at me, but this doesn't bother me much because I am imagining one of these good humans charging away from her post and grabbing those filthy mongrels by their necks and heaving them out the door and into a stream of oncoming traffic where they will be smashed to the consistency of ground chuck by a caravan of Bekins moving trucks while I am being invited, led back by the hand, to the cool, moist room behind the vegetable bin for private tour and a cup of tea and to tell her all about it.

But no one else seems to notice the dogs. I feel ashamed to ask help for something that doesn't bother anyone else.

I push the cart to the deli. I'm heading for the cheese section but one of the dogs throws herself against the cart. It swerves, first against a little old lady with a carrier basket who glares at me, I apologize, then to the destination they intended: the meat. One of the dogs hops up on her back legs, forepaws on the counter, and sticks her nose into the open refrigerated section. Bad dog! I shout, Down! The old lady spins around and, pursed-lipped, glares at me.

Sorry, I mumble.

She shakes her head and huffs down the aisle. Meanwhile, another pair of dogs—there's many more now than the trio I left home with—are standing up over the cooler, nosing at the flanks and legs, the joints and bones and cheeks. One of them grabs a particularly juicy thigh in its teeth and hoists it up into the air.

Bad dog! I screech again. Put that down! I grab the package from its mouth. The plastic rips and blood spews on the shelf of spices above the counter, on the floor, my clothes, including my shirt which is, was, white.

The big muscular deli woman, having heard the

ruckus, lumbers out of the back room wiping her bloody hands on her bloody apron. She sees the open package in my hands, the drops of blood all over the counter and me. She doesn't see the dogs. Then I don't either. I look beneath the cart and peek around the potted plant display but the dogs have scattered.

Can I help you? the deli woman asks.

This, um, package fell apart, I mumble.

Uh-huh, she answers, skeptically, until she catches herself. Gosh, she says, Sorry. Well, let's fix that up for you.

She takes the dripping package from me, courteously refraining from commenting on the tooth marks in the meat, and offers to cut me a fresh piece. I'm so flustered I can't say anything, much less that *I* don't want the damned meat, it was the dogs. She calls a kid in an apron over to clean up the mess then goes to the back and whacks off a hunk.

I don't know where the dogs have hid but when I find them I'm—I'm—I don't know what I'm going to do.

The deli gal comes back. When she hands me the package, I mutter thanks and try to tell this big, kind, understanding human that it wasn't me, it really was the dogs, but I just stand there with my mouth agape.

Are you OK, Miss? She leans over the counter toward me.

I nod yes like an idiot until I can stop myself. N-no, I say. I clench my teeth to force the words. It—was—n't—me.

She squints at me, puzzled, then slowly, when she's understood, says kindly, I understand, I understand, Hon, and leans across the counter and pats my hand.

I drop the package in the cart and push on down the aisle.

I go to the vegetable section, where I doubt my meat-mad dogs will find anything they want. The extremely cute vegetable girl—I see her from behind, the tie of her apron is tied *perfectly*—is spraying the spinach and lettuces. Everything looks so fresh and clean! So wholesome and delicious! I touch the smooth firm flesh of nectarines, the shiny skins of apples. I breathe in deep the pure green scents of celery and cilantro. The dogs stand upright, cross their forepaws, roll their eyes and tap their feet impatiently. I try to think of the name of that weird parsley so I can ask the vegetable girl something intelligent. But as soon as this thought enters my head the dogs, who eavesdrop on my brain, snarl, Bad Girl! Bad Girl! I clap my hand across my mouth in shock then spin around to face them but they're not there. I kneel down to look beneath the cart. The utterly cute vegetable girl is looking down at me concerned. Can I help you?

I stumble up.

Did you say something?

I try to think of something that sounds like, rhymes with, Bad Girl, Bad Girl, something one would casually say in a grocery store. I cough a couple times though it even sounds fake to me. I point to my neck as if I've got a horrible cold. The vegetable girl pretends to believe it. She smiles understandingly, the way she would with any social service case. I don't get any vegetables.

I push my cart as fast as I can to the paper products and

feminine hygiene aisle. I'm the only person there. I take this as an opportunity to compare the prices and sizes of the tampons and napkins, the applicators, scenteds and nonscenteds, with and without baking soda, squares per foot, thickness, quilting, ecological impact of packaging, and animal testing that went into the development of this product (cruelty to *some* animals being a selling point in my book), innies and outties, plugs and pads, torpedoes and rags, minis, maxis, supers, heavy days, lite days, panty liners, bullets, mattresses and so forth, when I hear a distinct and loud and collective snicker behind me then a veritable chorus singing: PEEEEE-YEEEEW! I spin around.

The dogs, several dozen now, are standing upright in a semicircle around me. They go up in layers like a short-on-talent, long-on-enthusiasm local chorus that performs on the bleachers at the high school gym. They're in their choral garb but instead of holding their music in front of them, they are pinching their noses closed and snorting PEEEE-YEEEEEW! A bunch of brats with the world's oldest pottie joke.

God damn you! I yell. I flap my arms at them when around the corner of the aisle comes a mom and a pair of pimply preteens. The dogs disappear like magic. The family stops abruptly when they see me flailing. I lower my hand to cover my mouth and pretend to cough then smile wearily at them like I'm some poor, sensitive, uncomplaining soul afflicted with both Tourrette's syndrome and consumption. They smile back, not sadly as I'd hoped, but nervously. Mom ushers them down the aisle.

When I stand in the line at the register, I try to catch

someone's eye. I want to lean over and whisper, They're here, but the only thing I can say when the cashier tells me, Have a nice Day! is Thanks!

The dogs push the grocery cart to the parking lot, which is not the way I usually go home. I usually turn left at the door and walk on the sidewalk carrying everything in a huge backpack and a zillion over-the-shoulder eco-bags because I don't own a car.

Not only can I not afford one but, more importantly, the dogs won't let me. They know that if I had a car, a ton or thereabouts of hurtling metal, glass and speed, what I would do. For starters, in the dead of night, I'd catch the dogs, I'd freeze them in the headlights, blind, and then I would not, like a good girl, stop. No, I'd keep moving. I'd accelerate. I'd slam into the pack of them then each and every single one as an individual. Then I would not drive off. I wouldn't do a measly little hit and run. No, I would hit and stay. I would admit responsibility, I'd relish it. When I heard them slam against the chrome, when I saw the jaws and teeth and guts exploding like confetti and felt the crunch of ribs beneath the tires, I would screech to a halt then yank that baby into reverse and back over and over and over them. Then I'd drive to the mountains, to the edge of a cliff where a car shouldn't go, where no one should go and I would —

The dogs won't let me.

Despite the fact that they *love* cars. They love chasing them and barking at them and yipping at them and peeing on their hubcaps. They've got that stupid, gleeful, blissful way they hang their heads out of fast-moving open windows and face the hurtling wind with their big ears flapping.

At first it would sound a bit like walking on gravel. Then it would sound a bit like walking on grapes. I'd make them smooth as pastry dough, the tire marks as lovely as the patterns of a very fussy pastry chef. (No lumps.) In the pure illumination of the headlights, I would see the wet, red, flattened mush.

But the dogs in their wise wisdom will not let me drive.

Conveniently, mysteriously, a cabbie is waiting for us at the store curbside. The dogs push the grocery cart and me toward it. I don't want to take a cab. I can't afford it! I know Miss Dog won't reimburse me. It's my job to haul their stuff, to be their beast of burden.

But the pups insist. One of them opens a door and shoves me inside. They yank the bags from my hands and back and throw them in the open trunk. When I hear the groceries thunk I pray the eggs and milk remain intact. The dogs leap in around me, a string of fluid black. Their claws scrape on the upholstery and their dirty paws make prints. I can already hear Miss Dog blaming me. Most of them scramble over the seat to flop into the back. A trio of them stay up front with the cabbie who doesn't seem to notice them at all.

I don't want to leave the store. I want to stay where humans come and go, where I am within shouting distance of someone.

The cabbie starts the car. I don't tell him where to go, he's already on the way. Of course, I sigh inside myself, Miss Dog must have called him.

The dogs squirm and whine and paw at one another.

They won't sit still. I remember the things my teachers and Girl Scout leaders used to say to us monstrous kids when we were on outings and say the same to them: OK you guys, settle down. I know you're excited but we're not at the playground.

We're crammed together in the back. The dog who is sitting next to me grins at me widely. Her teeth are long and yellow and the tip of one of her fangs glistens with a pearl of wet like in a Disney cartoon or an ad for bathroom cleanser. I swear I hear that bright little *ping!* of a grade school music-class triangle. Then she stretches her neck up and howls a long loud howl of anticipation. A couple of her chums join in, then all of them. I put my hands over my ears and they howl even louder. I try to shout above them, I'll tell Miss Dog! When we get home I'll tell her how awful you all behaved! I'll tell—

The dogs burst into raucous laughter. The cabbie, in his wide-brimmed hat and dark sun specs, stares silently, straight ahead. The dogs shake their heads and giggle. My threatening them is ridiculous. They know as well as I I can't do anything.

The cab jolts from the parking lot then does no less than seventy-five through this quiet leafy neighborhood. Bikers squeal away from us. Old folks with walkers tumble down and skateboarders drop their jaws in admiration as we barrel through the streets. The dogs stick their heads, their grinning mugs, out the open windows. Their ears flap in the roaring wind. They yowl, they spit, they slaver and slobber all over me with glee.

I cower underneath them in the back seat, mortified.

14

GLASS... IN WHICH IS ILLUSTRATED PRUDENCE

Sometimes when I am with them, and we're just about our businesses, industrious for them and still for me, sometimes when I would least expect, I see them like we're new.

As if there was, I was, another person, separate, outside,

who has not lived with them, with us, who does not know. This normal person passing by and glancing in, the glass is dark, can see. She sees a tiny studio apartment, girl and dogs. She sees the sweet companionship, the comfy domesticity. They look like anyone to her. They look like her.

Then other times, sometimes the same, when we're about our business, they're around me in a circle getting smaller, not them as individuals, the circle, closing in, and growling. I'm going down, I'm on my knees, my head is teary, hot, and someone passing by outside sees in the glass and sees this small apartment, girl and dogs, and thinks, Why does she stay like that with them? Why does the girl not leave?

Because each hate and fear she knows, each longing, every clutch of love, and that which turns desire into need abides in them.

15

gIRL...IN WHICH IS ILLUSTRATED FAITH

No one else has seen them so I must have made them up. I tell myself I made them up. I blame myself. I tell myself I can and must as easily unmake them.

I leave the apartment and duck into a phone booth to change. I put on my blue and white checked dress. I look as fresh as a Kansas girl. (It's true, in fact, we lived there once.) My hair is gold and my cheeks are pink and my hands are clean and my nails are clean. I haven't bitten them, no one has, and my legs are spotless, bruises gone, and I'm wearing my white anklets and my eyes are bright and blue and I'm as pretty as a picture but not too pretty, not-asking-for-it pretty, just nice pretty. I am not wearing that cape and that covering hood and it is not the woods, not dark and not where Grandma lived, poor helpless old bat, no, it is not the woods, it's safer, light, entirely safe and open, it's the suburbs, it's my neighborhood.

As an extra precaution nonetheless, for one can never be too safe, I also wear extra layers, a clean white under-shirt and clean white panties. Then additionally, as an extra, extra precaution, because they say anonymity somehow allows them to do it, I write my name on a name tag and pin it on the collar of my dress. This time I make my name be Pollyanna.

I skip along rolling my bright pink hula hoop. My cheeks are rosy, my eyes are blue. I have cute little knobby knees and tiny snow-white wrists. My skin is clean and white and pure.

It's sunny out and the cloudless sky is blue. Moms and dads and children picnic in the park. The dads wear bar-be-que aprons over their short-sleeved shirts and slacks. Sweet chubby well-behaved grandmas with curly white hair and uncloudy eyes and pink healthy unmarked skin and hair sit upright unaided unrestrained continent, neither drooling nor peeing on themselves in picnic chairs. The moms wear nice dresses, belted at the waist, while they pour Koolaid for their adorable kids. Harmless little puppies, those cute fuzzy happy dumb-looking ones like from the old TV show *Please Don't Eat the Daisies*, frisk around the babies who happily play patticake with protective elder siblings on homemade-by-healthy-Grandma quilts. (I miss her terribly, terribly.) The puppies are little too, so small and harmless. I can see the homemade banana cream pie Mom's set in the center of the table for dessert and I can smell hamburgers and hotdogs grilling and they smell delicious, smoky and savory, though also somehow curious, with a slightly cloying unfamiliar sweet scent. Perhaps it's Dad's special hot bar-be-que sauce. I wave to them all as I roll my hula hoop by and they wave back. They are, we are, each one of us, polite and clean and well-behaved and good.

I'm whistling because I'm just like everyone. Nothing bad has happened, or if it has, it's over now for no one else has seen them —

Then I do.

I'm skipping along with my hula hoop. It's red. It rolls away. I run to catch it. It goes around so fast it's dizzying. It looks like a scene from a kids' cartoon, like a blurry circular saw. The dumb looking *Please Don't Eat the Daisies* puppy leaps off the kiddie blanket and runs after me. (I see this scene, mysteriously, from the back of my head.) But I keep my eyes on the hula hoop. It goes faster and farther away from me, so I run faster, farther. My legs look like that old cartoon. I see this, too, from somewhere else. My legs pump a blur like a circular saw. My blue and white checked dress is whipped against me. Now I look like one of those space age or World War II movies where the pilots are pressed by the G-force and the skin of their faces is pressing in, their mouths are pulled back around their teeth, the blood's coming out of their noses and mouths. But I'm not bleeding there. Not there, not this time.

For something catches me.

I fall.

The dog clamps its teeth into my right calf. I twist to pull away. The dog holds tight. Its coat is white and curly and, aside from what it's doing, the dog looks nice. I grab my leg and pull it away. The dog comes with it. I pray the dog will drop my leg. It doesn't. It yanks my leg again. It shakes its head back and forth in ecstasy. My leg goes with it, back and forth. Blood sprays on the dog's white curly head. It sprays in my eyes and nose. My vision blurs with blinding pain and I see the dog's white curly head turn black. It turns from playful pup to Doberman then back to puppy again. Each twist of my leg it turns from one dog to the other.

This can't—this can't be how it is —

Try again.

Think positive. Here I go. Again.

I'm skipping along with my hula hoop.

No. I won't skip. The motion might attract them like a bull. I'm walking slowly, cautiously, circumspectly. (That's better.) My skin is fresh and clean and white and doesn't smell of anything and though I have an adorable smile, it is a careful smile and could not, by any reasonable person, be mistaken for inviting or provocative or asking-for-it and though my skirt is loose and sort of short, it is tastefully cut, neither suggestive nor revealing. The day is sunny and cloudless blue and I am in the park with lots of people around, moms and dads and children picnicking and bar-be-queing and I roll my hula hoop slowly, carefully and I can smell hamburgers and hotdogs and other things grilling and they smell delicious, smoky and savory, but also somehow cloying, sweet, curious, but getting familiar by now and I shout hello and wave and they turn to see who's waving and they wave and shout hello and smile at me and I see their —

Teeth.

How can I be such an idiot? The shouts hello are growls, the waves are swiping paws. The puppy on the blanket with the baby isn't small, it's huge, and it takes the kid's head in its teeth and shakes it back and forth. Then all of them are bursting from their human clothes. Their pale skin gets hairy and dark. The flesh of their hands is busted apart and claws poke through. Their smiles broaden to long sharp fangs. Their foreheads squash, their eyes get black, their ears grow into points. The meat that's sizzling on the grill is human arms and legs.

No one else can see them because there's no one left to see.

I try to run. My skirt is ripped. I trip and fall. I try to cover my eyes and face. They tear me apart with their teeth. They eat my brains.

16

HEART...IN WHICH IS ILLUSTRATED

RIGHTEOUSNESS

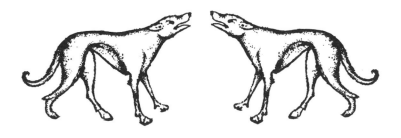

They let me out to go to work, to bring home bones. I used to look forward to going out to get away from them.

But then when I wasn't with them, how I thought of them! Everywhere I went and everyone I saw and everything I did, I thought of them.

For as much as I wanted to get away, I missed them. It got so I got restless, when I was away, to get back home to them.

Then after a longer time, I felt like whoever looked at me could see them, though I knew this was impossible.

Then I wanted someone else to see, and then I was ashamed somebody would.

Then one night I was at the bar and I was listening to some pretty girl, but only half listening. I started drifting off and I slipped in my chair and thought I'd kicked her under the table and mumbled I'm sorry and she said, What?

I said, I'm sorry I kicked you.

She said, You didn't kick me.

But I had felt something so I looked under the table and it wasn't her foot I had kicked, it was a dog. Curled up as sweet and comfortable, as cozy as if it were in its living room next to my slippers. It looked almost asleep. But one eye, open, stared straight up at me and winked.

I must have groaned.

What is it, this girl asked.

Nothing, I said.

Then we had another round or two and closed out the bar and I brought her home.

On the way back to my apartment maybe we talked some small talk but I don't remember. I wasn't paying attention. We went in my building and up the stairs. When I stuck the key in the lock to my apartment I suddenly shivered. I gave this girl a pathetic little smile. Was I hoping she'd see my hesitance and remember suddenly that she had an appointment somewhere else? (It was

2 AM). Or was I really expecting that I could just breeze out and haul a human being back to my place?

Before I could do anything this girl had pushed the door open and slipped into the room in front of me. Her hair brushed my face. I could smell the smoke from the bar. She flipped on the overhead light bulb. I flinched. I didn't want her to see the dogs. Or have the dogs see her.

She tossed her baseball cap and jacket on the back of the chair and sat on the bed. I sat next to her and she kicked off one of her shoes. The laces clicked when they fell to the floor and I gasped.

What's the matter, she said.

Nothing, I lied. I looked at the floor.

Well, come on, she said impatiently. (She was the kind of girl I used to like.) She kicked off her other shoe and I heard another click.

I looked down and saw a claw sticking out from beneath the bed. The girl was unbuttoning her shirt. I grabbed her shirt and threw it over the claw. Which was now attached to a paw. Which was coming out from beneath the bed. The girl laughed like my pulling her shirt off was fun.

She put her hands on my shirt to take it off.

No, I said.

Shy? She snickered as if this was also fun.

No, I tried to say again, but she grabbed the bottom of my shirt and lifted it over my head. I yanked my shirt off and dropped it on the black muzzle nosing out from beneath the bed. I held my breath. She lifted her t-shirt over her head. The skin of her shoulders was even and smooth. Her collar bone was exquisite. I looked down and the muzzle threw my shirt off. The girl put her hand on my neck. Another paw was beside the first.

Come on, she said and then was on me. The dogs stirred and I pulled away.

Relax, she said.

It was such a classic line they laughed.

Relax, she said again, a bit impatiently.

I stared at the floor. The paws and muzzle had slipped back beneath the bed. What fucking game were we playing?

She pulled me. There was a growl.

Come *on* already, she snarled. She pulled at my belt loops. I closed my eyes and we fumbled around. I heard our hands swish over each other. I heard the opening of mouths, the clack of teeth, the rustles of the dogs. We put our mouths against each other and opened them.

Open-mouthed, the puppies gasp. They're eager to play, they're having fun. They're playing Punch and Judy, that hokey old where-will-they-pop-up next routine. I feel her mouth, this girl's, and her hands, but I can't see her, my eyes are closed, but I see the toothy muzzles and pointy ears, the long, pink lolling tongues. Their goofy mugs burst through the paper backdrop on stage. They swing down from a ceiling bar and pop up through a trap door, from inside a traveller's trunk, from underneath the bed. And I am, as always, every time, the wide-eyed fool, the idiot, the clown. My floppy, giant-toed shoes trip me and my dirty, white-gloved hands are thumbs that poke out from my hips. I can't lift them away, I'm tipped off balance. I know the bowler hat that crowns me like a pin will not protect me from the bucket of whatever is above the door that I'm about to walk through. I wish someone would stop me but I don't.

Hey, this girl says, Whoa, and squeezes me by the shoulders.

My head is down, my eyes are closed. My body's still moving toward her as if it hasn't heard.

Stop, she says firmly and pushes my body away.

I pull myself away and roll over on the bed. The room rolls over. I'm afraid I'll step on one of the dogs and piss it off but I find the floor with my feet and, swaying, stand.

I open my eyes and look at her. She's holding her hands in front of her as if to keep me away. I want to tell her something but I can't. I shake my head and close my eyes again and I see the dogs beneath the bed like the kids backstage who play the angels in the Christmas show. But then it's not the cover of my bed they hide behind, it's a curtain, and they're on stage, and the curtain's open and it's their cue, they're front and center and performing. As am I.

The place is packed. (Admittedly, with comps. We had to drag them in.) I'm doing my desperate, sweetest, heart-felt best but I can't convince them. The dogs don't care that my role is meant to make them cry; they're laughing! They're shaking, doubled over, tears streaming out of their jolly, squinting eyes. They're a bunch of vaudeville comics yucking it up over a corny prank I am the object of. They're rolling around on a garishly lit stage as big as the Palladium. I try to picture a hooked cane popping out from stage right and dragging them back by their necks — no — I try to picture that hook of a cane inside their ribs and hooking their pebble hearts. But I can't make that picture come. I can only see them chortling, their skinny eyelids squeezing out their tears.

I look behind the footlights and into this girl's eyes as if I could tell her.

I take a deep breath. Then with the stiffness of a miserably overcoached pre-teen in a spinster's elocution class, I pronounce: I-guess-you-should-go.

The dogs howl! They burst! Their jaws stretch wide. Their eyes pour giggly tears. They stamp their two-toned shoes. Have you ever heard such a funny thing, they ask themselves in stage-whisper asides. I'm better than the travelling salesman, the farmer's daughter, I'm better than Take-My-Wife-Please. They slap their knees, take their bowlers off and fan their sweaty faces. They stick cigars in their mouths and clap and clap and clap.

Down, I think to myself, *Down*.

Their shoulders shake. They pull wrinkled hankies from their oversized pinstripe suits and wipe their piggy eyes. They blow cigar smoke up into the overhead lights.

The girl is staring at me. I wonder if she can hear the dogs.

I say each syllable slowly, like talking with a foreigner. No, not to a foreigner, but like I *am* a foreigner: I-guess-you-should-leave-now, I squack. *Stop! Down!* I shoo them away.

They kick up their heels and raise their skinny noses and their horrible flabby jowls in boisterous song.

I stumble back to the chair this girl has thrown her jacket across.

The girl doesn't move.

Their ears perk up. Their hats tip awry. They pat their bowlers on their heads with their white-gloved paws.

Please, I say. I hold out her cap and jacket to her.

They put their forepaws around each other's shoulders and sway back and forth.

She takes the jacket. Its weight lifts from my hands like a promise I never meant to keep. Their ears are up. Their bowlers bump into the bottom of the bed.

That was quick, the girl says, raising an eyebrow.

The chorus line of dogs sways back and forth, clicking their claws to a sloppy, sentimental song.

So long, the girl smirks.

Their hankies wave good-bye in a Busby Berkeley wave.

She puts her jacket on. I hand her her baseball cap. She taps it on her head, tugs the bill down a bit over the back of her neck and looks at me. I shrug. She gets this look on her face like I'm a total jerk then shakes her head and walks to the door. The dogs press their hankies to their muzzles and blow. I don't even try to say anything because the dogs are blowing extremely loud, high-decibel, fart-sounding honks into their hankies. Who could hear anything beneath such racket?

The girl is at the door.

Stay, I'm thinking, *Please*. I don't say anything.

She puts her hand to the doorknob. The dogs grab forepaws and snap their feet together and stretch all the way from stage right to stage left and bow as one. She turns the door handle. One of the dogs, an especially beautiful one, breaks from the chorus to come forward, lift her paws to left and right, the pit, up to the balcony, the light booth. She is a gracious, gorgeous star and she is giving humble-seeming thanks to her loyal, hard-working, adoring company. She opens the door to let herself out. She pauses. Someone runs up with a dozen beautiful long-stemmed roses for her. She smiles a rapturous, yet modest smile, then clasps her hands above her heart. She accepts the flowers and bows. She doesn't turn. She pulls the door closed behind her. The curtain falls. My door clicks locked. There's a click of claws then thundrous applause. Their feet stomp in enthusiasm. Her feet pad down to the end of the hall. Backstage, they're opening and closing dressing room doors, they're shifting sets. She opens the door at the end of the hall. I hear it close behind her.

I see her. I can see the girl in the back of my head. She's on the landing, then going down the steps to the first floor. I know just when her hand will touch, it touches, the door. She lets herself out back. I see her step into the alley, into the dark wet night outside, into the rain. Backstage the dogs are peeling off this night's make up, pulling off their white, white skin with cold cream. She pulls her jacket around her tightly, crosses her arms and lowers her head against the drizzle. In the alley outside the stage door, fans are waiting for an autograph or to touch the hem of a garment or to see the fancy car the chauffeur drives away. She walks out the alley to Howell. There's so much competition for a cab this time of night. Most of the audience has to walk. She crosses 17th then 16th. The dogs stream out of the theater in their tuxes and tails and formals and furs. She gets to 15th and waits for the Night

Owl bus to take her back to her apartment where she will fix herself a cup of tea. The dogs settle down in smart cafes where fine linen napkins are tucked beneath china dessert plates and fancy patterned silverware and coffee cups with saucers. I step to my door and double lock the lock. They order coffee and liqueurs and cakes and bones. I sit down in my chair and take a deep breath. I lift my hands in front of my face; they're shaking. The dogs chat about their stocks and art and chat each other up: Your place or mine? A penthouse at the Ritz?

I look at the bed, the dark two-inch line beneath it. At first there's nothing but I blink and see a nose. Then a paw. Another paw. Then more of the head, the lips and jaw. The black spotted flap of the gums. The shiny eyes. Then the two brown dots above the eyes, the square block of the top of the head, the two stiff ears. Then the forepaws stretch and the claws click and she scrambles out. Then there's another set of paws and nose. Another. Another. Another. The pack scrambles out from under the bed.

I expect them to be jocular—they've had a lot of fun tonight—but they are not. They're quiet and attentive, reverent. Reverently they arrange themselves in a semicircle then in concentric semicircles behind that one. They sit straight and still, their backs aligned, feet together in front of them, their sharp ears back, their dark eyes sad as Greco's saints. Like those saints they're looking up. So I do too.

To the overhead light, a bright bare bulb. The one that's shed its wretched self on my abominations.

I look up and gasp, then clasp my shaking palm to my—empty?—chest.

For hanging from the fixture it is not a light, it is a
rope. And from that rope, a thing of red. The dogs look
up at it with longing. It's a piece of meat.

It's a part of me. A part of me is hanging there, the
toughest little nut of me my dolorous, my *verté* my heart.

It's me inside that rope, which is a noose. I'm standing
but I can't see what I'm standing on. On nothing? Air? On
fear of them? The rope is pulling, slowly, I am stretching
up my neck, my heart, to keep from choking.

The dogs are underneath, intent and ready.

I'm choking. I cannot stay up. The noose is tight
around my throat, around my foolish heart. But also, now,
I'm someone else. I also wear a hangman's mask, a mercy
mask, a mask of shame so I can't see my face.

The dogs are waiting underneath. They know I can't
go on like this.

I look out through my hangman' s hood and see them
and am terrified.

But then I think how this could be a comfort: I could
be released.

The dogs have always known what I've not wanted to.
The loyal, patient, prescient dogs were sent to teach, to
help me know and do what I was meant.

I hear us say the words to me. I hear us tell me, *Jump,
you sucker. Jump, you fool pathetic child, Jump.*

And so I do. I jump.

17

WOUND...IN WHICH IS ILLUSTRATED CONTRITION

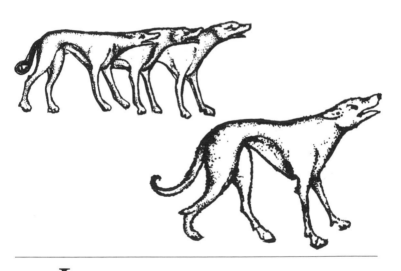

I wake up on the floor. I'm wet. The rug is cold. I try to lift my head but my neck is limp. My eyes roll down to look. I'm flat as a sack, a deflated balloon. I'm wet inside and little bumps of air or goo or something are beneath my skin. There's nothing solid in me and my mouth is sour. I roll my eyes so low they hurt and see there in the middle of my front, the place where it was hacked from me. I try to lift my hand to close the wound but I'm as weak as paper. I can't move.

Oddly enough, it doesn't hurt.

Thank God, I think, Thank Jesus. I close my eyes and think, although I do not know to whom: *Please.*

I think I'm about to cry but I don't want the salt to sting me. Then I feel something cool on my face. A muzzle holding a cool damp cloth.

I feel a nose behind me, nudging against the skin on the lump of my head. I feel paws and the tug of teeth along my arms and legs but it feels gentle. I feel me lifted like a sack. The contents of the stuff inside me shifts. Some dogs scramble beneath me to hold up my back and butt. They carry me.

I billow like a parachute above them. They hold me carefully as a flag, like a something they hold dear. When I feel my head fall back, somebody catches it.

I try to keep my mess in the middle, the way you try to keep a puddle in the center of the pool cover you're dumping the rain water out of but I tip and hear it slosh and splat on the floor. I hear the puppies slip. I try to mumble Sorry to them but no one grumbles. I hear some uncomplaining someone clean my mess.

They carry me in a solemn, slow procession. They try to keep me even but it's difficult. Suddenly, the features of my face slide around like a cubist portrait. It feels horrible, like my bones are melting. One of my eyes slips sideways so I can sort of see what's happening around me. It looks like something from one of those history books I used to love when I was a kid, a book about faraway and long ago, with beautiful color pictures and modern line drawings of how it was back then. Everyone wore their Sunday best, long black robes and red velvet capes and gold and amazing headgear, and the rooms they were in were airy and high and had deep-colored stained glass windows and light streamed in and everyone moved that slow, solemn way and had wise dark eyes and everything smelled wonderful, like incense, and it was beautiful and everything was going to be all right, everything was going to be fine.

But I can only see like that a little bit because suddenly I'm zoom-lensed back where I really am. I'm looking up at the ceiling, which I notice could use a coat of paint, and I'm hot and cracked and everything smells like blood and I'm sticky and crusty. They carry me, a solemn sad procession, to the bathroom.

Some big bruiser hurries a bunch of puppies out of the tub. (They love playing in there, slipping down the sides and batting the faucet drips.) Another dog springs up, shuts the drain and turns on the taps. Her claws glint. I hear water splash into the tub then smell the eucalyptus bath oil I only use for a treat when I've had an especially tough day. Someone closes the door. The bathroom starts to steam.

I slip down the side of the tub limp as a bag, a sheet, a skin. I can't really sink. The dogs carefully press me down to better immerse me, but they leave my nose and mouth holes above the water. Someone presses my chest down hard then lifts up very quickly, sort of like CPR, and my lungs pop open and air goes in and I suck it in then push it out: I'm breathing! (Perhaps my reanimation would more accurately be likened not to CPR, but to a john unclogged by a plunger.) When my lungs move the crusty patches on my skin begin to loosen. Water swooshes through my severed chest.

I'm embarrassed to have them handle me like this, but I'm too weak to protest. Fortunately, surprisingly, the dogs have excellent bedside—bathside?—manners.

Someone lifts my head above the water. My eyes moisten and I see better. I see the marble-cake swirls of red and black, the clots and strings of blood in the moving water. I bend my head a bit to see the open flaps of me. I'm pink and clean, the blood is no longer running.

I don't understand.

I try to think of nothing. I try to feel just the sweetness of the dewy-eyed, candy striped puppies who wash me.

After a while they pull me out of the tub. The dogs have covered the floor with the great big soft fluffy bath towels like I haven't had since I was a kid. Someone takes me from behind and pats me as gently as Grandma used to do and someone murmurs. Someone is kind to me and smells so sweet, like lavender water and powder and her hands are cool and kind and I am dozing, I am fading up to heaven until—

I jolt up in incredible, excruciating pain. I'm strapped in the bed, I can't get away, and the someone who was petting me has strayed her hand, her paw, her knife or prod, and it's against then in the hole where what was hacked away was hacked and I am screaming bloody pain like bloody murder.

My howling startles the dogs a bit but they've been trained and know what to expect. I thrash against the straps. They hold me down.

Miss Dog is above me looking down. Her muzzle's in a surgical mask, a long-nosed, specially tailored one, and her ears poke through a surgeon's cap. Her forepaws are gloved in latex. Her white-coated assistants keep me down while Miss Dog—pardon me, *Dr.* Dog—pours something in my body and it knocks me out.

It is with pity they knock me out.

They do it to give me respite.

I am out a long, long time.

While I sleep her elves are very hard at work.

They see the awful emptiness, the black hole of the heart, the hollow place that cannot be refilled.

By the time I awake, they've readied me: they've built me a prosthetic.

18

NIGHT...IN WHICH IS
ILLUSTRATED
OBEDIENCE

I am the balloon woman. Not that kind, not the kind who sells pretty colored air-filled toys to kids, though they are dear to me. No, I am the balloon woman. The dogs have rescued me.

Sometimes when I was in a room with someone, and

someone was saying something, part of me floated up and far away. I went away from where we were. I could not stay. I bumped into the ceiling because I wasn't watching where I was going because I was looking back because I wanted, how I wanted! to stay but I floated up. I waved, I tried to stay but couldn't. My shoulders and neck and back knocked up against the ceiling. I tried to swim back but I couldn't. For I was made of nothing, air. So I could not come back.

I can't.

Until they rescued me.

They rescue me.

Every night before I sleep, I sit in front of my mirror like an eighteeth-century lady at her toilet. My face is sagged and wrinkled because of what's seeped out of me during the day. It's only a little so no one else notices, but I am well aware that I'm diminished. I sit at the mirror and look at myself. Behind me, in my tiny room, I see the dogs. They're partying like in a couple of scenes out of Hogarth. Some of them are sprawled across a squat wooden table in a low-life tavern. Others tipple at high-backed, ornately carved chairs in a high-ceilinged drawing room. They're swigging from tankards or sipping from thin-stemmed crystal glasses. A trio of them takes turns sticking their manicured claws down the over-flowing blouse of a heavily made up, gap-toothed, very buxom mongrel. I can see the cracks in the cheap, thick powder this poor old cur has painted on to hide her sags and wrinkles. I try to look away from them, but even when I close my eyes I see them.

When the dogs have had enough of her, they return their attentions to me. They glide around me sly as rakes (the lower-class ones having fallen down to snooze beside their spit) bowing low, extravagant bows, and arcing their embroidered, perfumed hankies around my haggard face. They nuzzle me with their moist, cold muzzles and nip me with their shiny yellow teeth. I want them to get it over with, but I know not to rush them. I clench my teeth and hold my breath and try to not feel anything. I'm taut as a lampshade, stiff as a doll.

I try to not feel anything.

But I do. They lick me till I tremble and my holes and seams are opened and I collapse. The air inside me wheezes out. My poor head topples sideways then my back slumps down. My arms and legs and thighs get thin. They press me down until there's only a little air in me, then they put their mouths against my open holes and suck. They suck out the rods. When I'm deflated they grab me by their teeth and drag me into bed with them.

They lay all over, on top of me, I feel them walking over me. My insides press against myself. The dogs do what they will.

Thus every night they empty me.

Thus every single night they fill my bed.

Then every morning, each and every day, they make me ready. They do what they undid the night before.

When the alarm the dogs have set goes off, my neck jerks up like a licorice whip and my eyes, pickle bumps on the flat fan of my face, pop open. My unsupported skin is spread across the bed like putty. The dogs leap up and drag me to the bathroom. They slam me up against the tub. I slip over the edge like that watch in Dali's *Persistence of Memory*. I drape my rubbery hand over the faucet to try to coax the water, but of course my boneless flesh can't turn the faucet. The dogs, who are very extremely clean, as I am not, they tell me so, they don't know how I bear myself, assist. One of the dogs who has been panting, grinning by the door, skips up and turns the faucet with his teeth. He's young and fit, and oh, so much more agile than am I. In the filling tub I float like a plastic sheet. When the dogs are ready, they dunk me.

They "wash" me (that's what they call their rubbing, poking, paws) then squeeze me dry. A couple of them tease me, tugging me back and forth between them until one of them gets me in its teeth, hauls me back to the main room and drops me to the floor. Then I hear them snickering. Of all the things they get to do, I think they like it best when I ask them for it.

Every day, yes, every single day they make me beg. For what I hate the very most. But what they know, and I know too, I cannot live without. So I beg them, every day, to fill me. They get their daily victory, which is my daily shame.

I feel filthy.

The rods are leaning against the bed like mismatched crutches. The dogs knock them down and I, like a proto-

zoan, like the very lowest form of life, ooze myself over
the rods. The dogs find my holes and ram the rods back
into me. Down through my middle opening, two longish
rods for legs. Then up the same, a slightly shorter one: my
back. Then through my mouth: two medium rods for
arms. Then, finally, for my head and neck, a stump.

Sometimes, for fun, the dogs put the rods inside me
wrong—the long one up my neck so the soft spot in my
head nearly bursts, or two mismatched ones for my legs.
This makes me even more ugly and deformed and it also
hurts: the dogs enjoy it. Only when they've had their
laughs do they take the rods out and put them in again the
proper way. When the rods are finally in me right, the
dogs lick closed my seams and holes. Except my mouth,
which they let me open and close myself. The dogs get a
kick out of seeing the stupid things I can put in, and the
awful, stupid things I can make come out of it. I must
admit, the dogs are right: my mouth can do and say the
dumbest things. I finish by opening my mouth in a big
round "O" which looks like a cry of horror or alarm, or
perhaps of hope or ecstasy, and gulp in air. I gulp as much
as anyone can. I blow myself up like a balloon. I gulp until
my fingers and toes, my ears and nose and tips and points,
pop out. Then I take one huge and final gulp to seal the
place down deep inside my throat that keeps me in and
keeps the world out.

I teeter to the mirror where I sat the night before. I
always have to readjust myself. I press my tingling fingers
to the places I'm not right and pull and push. The canines,
who are perfect, sit around me and whisper to one

another. They comment about every inch of me—my
boring, pasty, milk-white skin, my sagging tits, my fingernails that can't scratch half as much as claws, my useless
teeth. They shake their gorgeous heads about my weak-
nesses and flaws. They bark to tell me how I should
improve myself. I try to do what they demand—to make
my eyebrows sharp and straight, or pull my nose more thin
and long, or color my larvae colored flesh. I try to make
me look like them; I can't.

The dogs have put a checklist by the mirror. They
make me stand up, naked, so the pack of them, around me
in a semicircle, can inspect me. I am on show, an auction
block, a grade-school spelling bee. Miss Dog, tall, thin, a
perfectly proportioned bitch, strides up beside me. She
stands erect on her firm hind legs. She's wearing pointy,
dark framed glasses and her ears are tied back in a prim,
tight bun. She holds a pointing stick. Briskly, militarily, she
sniffs. I try to stand at attention, but I'm a clunky, too big,
awkward kid, a slob. I try to straighten my horrible pos-
ture, but everyone knows I'm hopeless. Still, Miss Dog
must check the basics. There is a crisp click of her pointer
against the list as she taps the word "mouth." Then there's
my squeaky answer: Check.
Another click. (Eyes.)
Check.
Click, click. (Arms, left and right.)
Check, check.
Click. (Head.)
Check.

Click, click, click, cli— (Stomach, tongue, thighs, two hands—)

Yes! Yes! Yes!

Her slit eyes glare through her specs at me. I don't know what I've done wrong, then do, and burble out the proper word: *Check*, check, check.

Sometimes the dogs write cute things on the checklist like Head on Crooked, or Bloodshot eyes, The Shakes, and Miss Dog has pointed at the word and I have answered Check before I notice what it really says. All of them are class clowns; I'm the fool.

Miss Dog pokes me with her pointer. I lift my arms and turn my head from side to side so she can check behind my ears and neck. I'm so unclean. With her pointer she lifts my lips and checks my gums and makes me stick my tongue out. I see in her beautiful face how much I repulse her. When she has seen what she requires of me, she swats her whipping stick across my ass.

I shuffle, head bowed, shoulders stooped, to the closet. I have to be careful with my clothes. If I wore something with a pin it could prick me or a zipper could tear me open and I'd deflate. I'm safest in my ragged, soft old sweats. Miss Dog *hates* the way I dress, but allows it as a way to help prevent at least this one particular potential disaster. The puppies help me button and zip. It's so humiliating, at their young age! But they're so much more dextrous than I.

When Miss Dog nods the briefest nod, this is my permission to go out. I open the door as quickly as I can and close it as quickly too. I hurry away from my tiny room and I do not look back.

* * *

I try to get away from them. Sometimes I used to make it to the outside door. Sometimes I've even made it to the street. Long ago, I think, I could, almost, get near the end of the block. But now, and always, every time, the dogs remain with me. They run with me and stay with me. They mark my every thought. I want to get away from them, but know, as they know too, that I could never get along without them.

For every day they wake with me and every single night they fill my bed.

19

FAMILψ...IN WHICH IS
ILLUSTRATED
VALOR

This story comes to us from Edward Topsell's bestiary, *The History of Four Footed Beasts* (1607).

"The dogs of India are conceived by tigers, for the Indians will take divers females or bitches and fasten them to trees in woods where tigers abide. The greedy, ravening tiger comes and instantly devours one or two of them if his lust does not restrain him and then, being filled with meat, he immediately burns in lust and so limes the living bitches, who are apt to conceive by him. Thus come these valorous dogs, which retain the stomach and courage of their father but the shape and proportion of their mother.

"Of this kind were the dogs given to Alexander by the King of Albania when Alexander was going into India and were presented by an Indian whom Alexander admired. Being desirous to try what virtue was contained in so great a body, Alexander caused a boar and a hart to be turned out to the dog, and when he would not so much as stir at the dog, he turned bears unto the dog, and he likewise disdained them and rose not from his kennel. The King commanded the heavy and dull beast (for so he termed him) to be hung up. The keeper, the Indian, informed the King that the dog respected not such beasts and that, if he would turn out unto him a lion, he should see what the dog would do.

"Immediately, a lion was put unto him, and at the first sight of it, the dog rose with speed (as if never before he saw his match or adversary worth his strength), and, bristling, the dog made force upon the lion, and likewise the lion at the dog. The dog took the chaps or snout of the lion into his mouth, where he held the lion by main strength until he strangled it. Desirous to save the lion's life, the King willed that the dog should be pulled off, but the labor of men and all their strength were too little to loosen those ireful and deep-biting teeth.

"Then the Indian informed the King that, unless

some violence was done unto the dog to put him to extreme pain, he would sooner die than let go his hold. Whereupon it was commanded to cut off a piece of the dog's tail, but the dog would not remove his teeth. Then one of his legs was severed from his body, but the dog seemed not appalled. After that, another leg was cut off, and consequently all four. The trunk of his body fell to the ground, but he still held the lion's snout within his mouth. At the last, it was commanded to cut off his head, and after it was done, the bodiless head still hung fast to the lion's paws. The King was wonderfully moved and sorrowfully repented his rashness in destroying a beast of so noble spirit, which could not be daunted with the presence of the king of beasts: choosing rather to leave his life than depart from the true strength and magnanimity of mind. To mitigate the king's sorrow, the Indian presented unto him four other dogs of the same quantity and nature."

(ed, Malcolm South, Nelson-Hall publishers, Chicago, 1981, pps. 64–66.)

20

FOOD...IN WHICH IS ILLUSTRATED PENITENCE

Have a heart, she said. She sounded nice.

I could smell something. It smelled like food. I opened my eyes. She was holding a tray in front of me. It looked like food and I was hungry. That is, I thought I was hungry because I was empty and she was holding a tray of hors d'ouvres. There were all these little things on it. They were on little doilies, skewered with toothpicks. I shut my eyes and shook my head. I was having one of my headaches again. I pressed my fingertips to my right temple as if I could pull it out.

Have a heart, she said again. This time she didn't sound so nice; she was ordering me.

Oh, thank you, I managed to say. (Having nothing else to keep, I have tried hard to keep dear Grandma's manners.) I lifted my arm — it felt like a bag of sand — above the tray to take one of the things.

Um, what are they? I asked.

Not "they," she answered, "it." She snickered.

It was the morning after the day before.

I didn't remember much of the night, or getting home, though I remembered going out, pissed off and low, and I remembered, I regret, the place I would — and I should not — have gone.

She didn't tell me what it was. She sniffed in a superior way as if I was an oaf, a fool, an idiot. A boor who'd never heard the words "pâté," or "steak tartar."

Her nose was long and black and thin and at the pointed end of it was wet and it had two tremendous holes. There was hair on her upper lip and her lower lip was quivering, a smirk, and her huge, brown eyes looked huge and brown, for she was wearing a pair of glasses. I wasn't wearing mine. I don't know how I saw any of this . . .

She was wearing a starched, white napkin-like cap and

apron as if she was the servant girl! She was wearing short white gloves that had threads popping out of the seams. They looked cheap, like polyester. (Miss Dog requires *me* to wear the best: cracking stiff starched white linen and cotton).

Who does this girl think she is, I thought. With those shoddy gloves so cheap they are unraveling? Yeah, I thought, Just who the hell does she think she is to come into my apartment and —

She sniffed again. Her horrible long black nose quivered in her special way. She might be wearing different clothes, but couldn't disguise her attitude.

I didn't know why she was dressed in my uniform, which is ugly and humiliating on anyone but especially on me. To wear this clothing seemed so unlike Miss Dog, who is severe, in charge and cold and always looks down her tremendous nose at us. (That is, at me.)

I looked up at her. She was standing on her hind legs, and — Dear God forgive my noticing, I simply could not help myself — she had terrific legs. She was wearing my serving girl sensible pumps (how on earth did she fit into them!?!) The black dress, on her, was both provocatively short, yet somehow tastefully long. Miss Dog knew, she always knows, the way to have it both ways, her ways, every time. The apron she wore over the dress looked white as driven snow, pristine, like it had never borne the junk, the ketchup chocolate coffee jam or blood that I had spilt all over it. Miss Dog was perfect.

But then, and only because I was unable to take my eyes off her legs, I noticed the stockings had a run in them, a familiar run. I wondered why Miss Dog, though she could make the thing I wore and hated every day, my serving garb, which while I wore it looked like shit, that is the thing that it contained, look great on her, fantastic, fabulous, could not correct improve undo this single simple flaw: the run in my panty hose. Then I was curious. I thought about the panty hose. About how I got that run. How I got that run was—oh that's another story.

She offered me the tray again and said again, with the cloying, oily confidence of anyone who knows they always get their way, Have a heart!

I decided to try to play along. I put on my PBS cooking show voice and chirped, Why, thank you, Miss Dog! They look lovely! How exactly would you have prepared this little treat? En brochette? Or bar-be-qued? Or did you chop or cube or dice or boil or fry?

She didn't miss a beat.

I'm glad you asked, she answered with a smile. Her gums rose and trembled above her teeth. Her eyes got thin. She offered me the tray again and when I didn't reach for one she pushed the edge of the tray against my severed chest—oh how it hurt! I knew I'd better pick one up. I touched my thumb and finger to the curly cellophane top of a toothpick—I chose a red one—and lifted it. It was heavy.

Surely you know what you've chosen there, she chirped.

I did, I did, I do.

It was very extremely heavy and it dripped and smelled. I couldn't lift it to my mouth. I didn't want to do it. I closed my eyes. I felt the sweat and tears and whatever else, run down my face, my chest. I prayed inside so silently, though I do not know to whom, that she'd not make me do it.

I would not move the piece toward my mouth. I kept my mouth closed tight and hard.

Have a heart, she says again.

I feel sick. My head is pounding, my stomach roils. The air goes through my empty chest where it was taken out.

I said, she orders, Have a heart. It's yours, goddammit. Eat it.

I try to be strong, I try not to cry, but I can't help myself. My eyes start gushing tears and then my poor dumb mouth is blubbering. I try to talk to her, or tell or beg. Then—oh I am such an idiot—I say the stupid thing and then it's even worse.

My eyes are full, about to burst. I open them and when I cannot look away, she does it.

She puts the tray in front of me. My hand that holds the toothpick opens, drops it. When it hits the ground I hear the splat and there's the jolt. I gasp. My mouth falls open. Then, like some old slapstick movie with a pie, she slams the tray, what it contains, against my face.

I try to breathe. I open my mouth. I take it in. I bite.

21

HAMMER ...IN WHICH IS
ILLUSTRATED
MERCY

One night they have a party to celebrate something they don't tell me about. Needless to say, they don't invite me. They build stage sets to make my room look like an eighteenth-century salon. They saw and buzz and hammer and paint and make an incredible racket. They're so talented! I'm amazed at how they can wield a saw or a level or hammer with their paws.

When my apartment has been transformed—flocked wall paper, high-backed chairs, bevelled mirrors, chandeliers —they clean up their mess then get themselves all gussied up in period dress and declaim excerpts from the collected barks of some overrated, pretty faced, and much luckier than me, dog. They yip and yap and prance around like a bevy of poodles.

About 3:00 A.M. I whine, Jeez, guys. Do you think you could knock it off and let me get some sleep?

One of the tougher, wiry ones lunges at me, but before it reaches me, Miss Dog yanks it back by its neck. I hear it hack and sputter. Miss Dog calls her charges off and announces, in an unusually considerate tone of voice, that they shall retire to the powder room to continue their soirée. That is, they're going to leave the main room so I can sleep. Then, in a gesture I have never seen before, Miss Dog curtsys demurely at me. I ought to wonder what's up.

Uh, thanks, I mumble, not quite believing they're going to leave me alone.

Miss Dog nods her one brief nod and turns—in a perfect arc on her perfect toes—and trots in a dignified fashion to the bathroom. The pack follows her. They swish off, apparently forgetting, in their festive mood, that they haven't fixed me the way they do every night before I go to sleep. But I'm not going to remind them. I drag myself, for the first time in I can't remember how long, fully intact, and alone, into bed.

The bed feels huge and the sheets are freezing when I

crawl inside. My body feels clunky and heavy with everything still inside me, like I'm all elbows and knees. I try to
get comfortable.

From the bathroom I hear them projecting in clearly
elocuted stage barks. I pull the blanket over my head and
hope I'll get some sleep after they finish their performance. I twist and turn but I can't sleep. After the very,
very long performance, I hear them applaud and return
for god knows how many curtain calls. I pull my knees up
to my chest and press the pillow over my head. I hear their
suggestive husky growls and high-pitched squeals as they
pinch each others' stump-tailed asses. I roll over on my
stomach and try to be still. I hear the twists of the caps of
their cold cream jars, the jangling of metal as they hang up
their fey little rhinestone party collars. The show is over
but they're making just as much, though a different kind
of, noise.

I've had enough.

I sit up abruptly in bed. I lean over to flip on the bedside lamp so I can see the clock but instead of finding the
lamp my hand feels something wooden. It feels like one of
my sticks but it can't be because my sticks are still inside
me. I pick it up. It's heavy. In the stripe of light that shows
through the crack at the bottom of the bathroom door, I
see a big, blunt, solid hunk of metal on top of a wooden
handle. Evidently some pup had forgotten to put it away
after they'd constructed the set for their celebration. It's a
hammer.

I throw myself back down in bed, yank the covers up
to my neck and slip the hammer beneath my pillow. The

tips of my fingers feel the fine grain of the wood. It's so smooth compared to my splintery sticks. (The dogs get everything nice for them; I always get the cheapest.) I hold my breath and listen. They're giggling in the bathroom. I turn on my side, tuck my knees up to my chest and bunch the covers around me so that when they come crawl into bed with me, they won't feel what I'm hiding.

From behind the bathroom door, I hear the flush of the john, then their collective chuckle, then an absurdly loud stage whisper, Sssshhhhh!, louder than all of their twitterings. Then there's the click of the bathroom light shutting off then the opening of the door. I pretend to sleep then open my left eye a slit to spy on them. Miss Dog sniffs briskly to bring them to attention. She leads them single file on tippy-paws through the darkness. I see, through the skinny slit of my open eye, as perfect and even as waves lit by the moon, their silvery backs approach me.

I hear the click of a single, careless claw. Miss Dog spins around, raises her front paw to her lips and mimes a ferociously impatient Ssshh! I can make out a few irrepressible trembles of shoulders of puppies. Miss Dog shushes them and they line up by the bed. I'm still lying as still as death. I hope they think I'm asleep. There's a pause, like just before when the conductor lets fly her baton, then one by one, the cutest, most adorable pups spring up into bed with me. They turn in circles and snuggle down. Then the younger, middle-sized dogs spring up. Then the big monster ones. They are as graceful as dancers, as careful and lithe as sprites. I watch their lovely ribs and torsos and their slender, coal black legs.

The bedclothes sink as they cover me. Some of them smell so fresh and washed, and some like perfume and incense. They press against me, their backs to mine, or curled inside the crooks of my knees. Some of them settle easily, while others sniff a spot to check it meets their mysterious standards. Some pat an area with a single front paw, then walk around in a small, tight circle to stake their claim. I feel them lie on top and all around me. Then we adjust, as we always do, our bodies to one another. None of them seems to notice I'm solid, more than just my usual bed-time emptied skin. We settle, heads to shoulders, paws to thighs, the larger fronts around the smaller backs. Someone nuzzles my face as if she's going to lie in front of me. But, with the leaden swing of the sleeper I pretend to be, I knock it away. None of them react to this. I tell myself they think I am asleep.

Beneath my pillow I grip my fist around the handle of the hammer. Through my slightly open eye, I watch the bodies near me slip from wakefulness to sleep, from shallow dreams that make them shake, to sleep more deep than dreams.

There is a moment, after, having watched them fall so quietly, so sweetly seeming into sleep, I wonder if what I have planned to do to them, what I have planned because of what they've done to me, how they have beat me flat and emptied me, how they have stolen what there was of me, and what I let them do because I never could believe they really would, could be undone. That is, I wonder if I could, by not doing what I long to them, reverse the pure, relentless hatred I possess for them.

But I do not desire to forgive.

No, I desire, rather, to recall, and to repeat, the awful things that they have done. I want to do to them what they have done to me, repeatedly, and willfully, and horribly each day and every night.

I slip the hammer from beneath the pillow. It whispers when I drag it on the sheet. With my one half-open eye I see the dull black hammer head against the clean white sheet. The back of a dog shifts against my back. I draw my other hand from beneath the covers and put it around the hammer handle too. I grip it tight. For the next few seconds I don't hear anything.

Because in one true, fluid moment I rear up and lift my arms and smash the hammer down against the dogs. I lift again and smash again, and lift and smash again. They knock against me with their paws, they growl and spit around my face. The pups cry high pitched yelps of pain. I hear the crunch of skulls and ribs and the hard dull whacks of the hammer as I murder them.

Above me their mouths are open, I see their snapping teeth and their bloody gashes dripping on, accusing me. One of them presses on me and I grab its neck and squeeze. The harder I squeeze, the harder its paws bear down on me. The dog's growls turn to gurgles as I throttle it. All the rest of the living dogs, and the ones — oh god — coming back to life, press against my body and pin me down.

I kick and scratch against them in a visceral, animal instinct to survive. But suddenly, my hands held tight around this young dog's sputtering throat, I think, Why am I trying so hard to stay alive?

Then I think, I don't want to do this, I don't want to be like this. Why don't I let them do it? Get me over with.

I loosen my hands from around the dog's neck. The dog makes sputtery, coughing noises, but doesn't lunge at me. None of them lunge.

Do it, I hiss.

No response.

Get it over with.

The dog whose paws are on my neck loosens them, its mouth. All the dogs close their mouths. None of them move. When I swallow I feel the callouses of the paws against my skin. This feels, suddenly, tender.

Please, I whisper.

The dog's dark eyes look down at me. She cocks her head. I try to hold her stare, but my eyes are stinging. I close my eyes and ask what I have never asked, What do you want from me?

She doesn't say anything. I swallow and feel the paw pull away. The paws no longer press on me, they merely rest, as though a laying on of hands. My chest rises and falls. With every breath I feel the soothing paw and every breath I draw becomes more calm.

When I am breathing evenly I feel the paw lift from me. My skin feels cool where the paw has been. Then I feel a paw in the air above my face. It lowers and makes a stroke, then another, across my forehead. Then I feel, all up and down my body, the laying on of a multitude of paws. The dogs are saying syllables that I don't understand. They're murmuring together, each alone, then all a body, in response. I feel the pads against my eyelids, lips and chest. There is a final murmur then one by one, and then in groups, the paws lift from my body.

I'm lying still and quiet and my breath is calm. I hear the little pups down near my feet, then the bigger, older dogs, I slip from the bed. The ones I haven't wounded slip down easily; I hear the gasps and stumbles of the maimed.

When I open my eyes to look, the only dog still on the bed is the one whose neck I'd almost snapped. The dog is looking down at me. Its deep brown eyes look into me for seconds. Then slowly, sadly, longingly, it lifts its paws away from me. I feel the bed shift where it's moved, and it slips, as quiet and smooth as water, from the bed.

I wake alone. My nightshirt is stuck with sweat and blood. The blood isn't mine. I open one eye hoping the dogs won't notice I'm awake. A bunch of pups in red and white candy striper uniforms are bustling back and forth from the kitchen to the far corner of my tiny room with steaming bundles. From the kitchen I hear pots clanging and water boiling and I smell the fresh clean smell of steam. The candy stripers are carrying my sterilized socks and undershirts, to the convalescents' corner. The room is full of activity, suddenly as big as a hospital ward. I can barely see all the victims. The volunteers arrange shiny tubes of ointment on rectangular trays, and read inspirational verses, excerpts, no doubt, from the collected barks of some over-rated pup. Whatever they're saying, whatever I can't quite hear, sounds almost familiar. The fresh-scrubbed, eager, earnest dogs play cards or make puzzles with the wounded ones, or tuck them into terry cloth bathrobes. They chop their dinners into tiny bites. I watch the tender way they hold their fellows' broken paws and pat their heads and ruffle their ears and whisper their kind, comforting sounding syllables. There is such ease in their benevolence.

I try to pretend I'm still asleep. I don't want to face what I've done. But when one of the candy stripers waves a cup of coffee under my nose, I can't resist. I sit up in bed and take the cup. They all stop bustling and stand still and I can see what I have done to them, I see whom I have clobbered.

None of the dogs is missing, somehow. None of them has died. There seem, in fact, to be more of them. My violence has given birth to more. Lots of them are lying on the makeshift cots their fellows have constructed from my junk.

I do not want to look at them. I look down in my coffee cup and see there in the wet black pool, my face. I blow on the stuff and my image breaks. I imagine the way the dogs were broken beneath my hammering hand. I look up through the coffee's steam, through the cold brittle light of morning and I see what I have wrought: the puffy eyes and swollen cheeks, the brows of crusty blood. The bones that poke out, red and white and jagged, from the skin. I see the purple bruises and the yellow, veiny gashes which expose their red insides.

I try to look away from them, what they and I have done.

But I cannot.

For I am drawn to look at them, at their million blaming, knowing, begging eyes. I look and look away until their million eyes become one eye, and that great eye looks into me, as it still does, each day and every night, a way I cannot bear to see: relentlessly and patiently for-giving me.

22

R☉AD...IN WHICH IS ILLUSTRATED PATIENCE

I could not get rid of them. I had to leave myself. In the dead of that dark night I left.

They slept around me warm as milk. The room was dark. Then suddenly there must have been a passing car or cloud that broke, for suddenly the dark was rent. A thin white line of pale light illuminated them. I saw their whiskers tremble and their soft-as-velvet ears. I saw the pink unguarded belly, the unknowing open mouth. I saw the body twitch and clutch with dreaming. I saw the body rise and fall with breath. Then I could hear the breathing. A sound to which I had become accustomed and a sound in which I had found joy.

I touched the bare uncovered skin. Not hard enough to wake, but just enough to feel the warmth that had been known to me. For I had been with them, as they with me, in such a way and in such time that we could be right next to us and not disturb the sleep. I saw and I remembered how we'd curled around each other, how we fit.

I tried to not remember what the dogs and I had done.

I slipped out from the mounds of them. I snuck from bed and got my pack. I lifted it and felt, although I was afraid to look, for fear that they or someone else, oh anyone, I don't know whom, could possibly observe, what I was checking for and stop me. No one did. I felt the pack to feel that it contained what I had hid, although I think I'd carried it forever, at least, that is, since I was Grandma's girl. I heaved it up onto my back, I almost fell, not yet, not then, not ready then, the place was not, the spot, my temples throbbed, I stumbled and I headed to the door.

As I opened the door I heard something. Was it a click? A sigh? A cry? Was someone saying, Stay? Did someone ask? I turned. Did I then see a glint? A shine of moonlight on an open eye? Was someone watching? Did someone see me leaving but pretend, to spare another lie, to sleep? Did I then hear a rustling? A warning or a blessing or a plea? Was it goodbye?

I didn't know that night, though later learned, there is a way to see when it's the last time you will see her sleep.

You will remember everything. And every time when you think back, as more and more you will, you will remember more than what you knew. Then more and more you'll wonder how you could have been when you were there. Then how you could have changed, how you could leave and then become the thing you are.

I sneak out silent as a ghost. I tiptoe out the inside door and lock the lock behind of what was home.

The sky is black. The air is cold. I'd planned to walk, but a city bus is waiting just outside the building. Though this is not a regular bus stop, I don't question my strange fortune. When the door to the bus slides open, I get on.

The driver doesn't look at me or ask the fare. I slip on without paying. Inside the bus is warm and damp, a night-owl route full of sleepers. I take a window seat near the back and settle in. The road shines with a coat of wet and I hear the swish of our tires. I slide the window open. The air feels great. I stick my head out the window like a dog.

The city looks different than I remember. But of course I'm not used to being out this time of night. I'm not really used to being out at all any more. The streets are lit with a flat eerie light that seems to come from every-where and nowhere, as if we're underneath a dome.

Nothing looks real. There are the blue green lights of tattoo parlors, the flashing lights of an all-night movie house, the orange light of the clock above the door of a twenty-four hour diner. Out by the water a ferry arrives, its long low row of windows an island of slow moving light. When the traffic lights turn red we stop although there are no other cars. In fact I see no other people out at all.

The bus doesn't stop en route but goes straight where I am headed: the Greyhound Station.

When I step into the station it's so bright. No one else is there except the ticket clerk, a skinny, stoop-shouldered, dark-skinned somebody wearing a wide brimmed hat and sunglasses. Everything is quiet. I hear my feet on the floor as I walk and I remember Grandma's pleading, when I was a miserable kid, Don't shuffle, Pick up your feet!

At the ticket counter I shuffle though my backpack for my wallet. Before I can even ask for my destination, the clerk hands me a ticket envelope. When I open my wallet to pay, he waves me off with his black-gloved hand. I grab the ticket and scurry away, suddenly afraid, unreasonably, that he'll ask me to check my backpack and I mustn't.

On the envelope is the date, the gate, my name. No destination. I run to the gate where the bus is already waiting. I jump on and the driver sticks his black-gloved hand out to take the ticket. I don't ask where we're going.

I find a seat and hunker down. The air in the bus is stuffy and warm. I am exhausted. Though also, of course, relieved. Suddenly I feel about to cry and I think about turning back, but I cannot. I've hoped and wanted and needed this so long. I've waited for release, it seems, forever. But somehow I am also sad. I wonder if there's something I forgot or if, if only —

I feel like I'm about to cry again but I will not and I will not go back. I close my eyes and soon I am asleep.

I wake up sometime later when the bus comes to a stop. I hear passengers getting on. I keep my eyes closed and pretend to sleep so no one will ask if the seat beside me is free. The passengers boarding whisper. I can't catch what they say but they seem to be travelling in a group. They help each other with luggage and they freely and frequently trade seats and pass tinfoil and wax-paper-wrapped goodies across the aisle. (I open my eye a crack to see when I hear this.) They speak with curious accents. I wonder where they're from but do not ask.

After we've been on the road a while again and they have settled down, I peek out the window beside me. Everywhere is darkness all around. The only light is the flat pale smudge of what we cast.

The driver of the bus shakes me awake. I blink up at the black-gloved hand. I cannot see the face.

It's your stop, the voice says quietly.

The hand pats my shoulder then lifts away and the driver moves up the aisle.

I get up slowly. As much as I've looked forward to this end, as much as I've wanted it over with, when the time is here, I hesitate. I think I hear, behind me on the bus, a kid start crying. Then some old lady must comfort her; because she quiets.

I grab my pack and head to the front of the bus. Some passengers are getting off ahead of me. I stand behind them in the aisle while they adjust their hats and gloves and coats and gather their tattered bags. I wonder if they are as tired as me, or maybe they are frightened. For none of them, of us, will speak. They gather their things so lovingly, so solemnly, almost. I wonder, Are they refugees?

We get off the bus in the utter dark. The only light is the light of the bus, the pale waxy glow from the windows, the long white line of headlights and the blood-bright red of tail lights as it pulls away. I watch the red lights go until they're gone.

When I look around the foreigners are gone. I am alone.

I look down at my feet and I cannot see any road. I get down on my knees to look but it's too dark. I try to feel a pavement, track or footprint but there is nothing I can sense.

But I believe a road is there. There has to be, I tell myself. Something has brought us here.

I set my backpack on the ground and sit beside it.

I will wait for light.

23

RIVER...IN WHICH IS
ILLUSTRATED
GRACE

When there is light I see I've landed where I want.
I get up, brush the gravel from my jeans, slip the flask I
inherited from Grandma out of my backpack pocket and
crash into the woods. It only takes a minute or two to find
it: a spiffy snappy tin can of an Italian sports car. Just like

Grandma used to like! (And had that once . . .) I pull the
handy hanger from my pack, twist it apart just right, pry it
through the window and pull up the lock. (This is an older,
classier model.) I get in, hot-cross the wires, also the way my
Grandma taught, carefully, very gingerly, lay my backpack,
its dear, redeeming contents on the passenger seat beside
me, take another swig and giggle when the engine purrs to
life like somebody's kitten. I ease her into gear, accelerate
gently, and bump out of the woods onto Olympic National
Park Forest Service maintainence road number 1142a.

This is a rugged, rustic, unpaved road, upon which
only are allowed suitably high-riding, four-wheel-drive,
all-terrain vehicles. Hah! Those wimps don't know how
to live!!

Once out of the trees I crank her up and floor it,
leaving, I assume, though I do not look back to see, a burn
of rubber in the smoking dirt. I barrel as fast as this baby'll
go. And then some.

The woods blur by alongside me. My ratty hair blows
in the wind, across my eyes. Sometimes, of course, this
means that I can't see, but I'm not bothered. In fact, I
laugh. Then take another pull from Grandma's flask.

I peel up to a lookout spot, a place I've always loved
but didn't know why. I stop the car and throw another
swig or three back then look. Below me I see Lake
Cushman. It looks surreal with all its black tree stumps
sticking out. I see Mount Elinor, which I climbed one
cold early morning many years ago. I remember the
crunching of snow underfoot and the firm smooth way it
felt. I remember the snow and the taste of a river that was

the clearest, coldest water I have ever had, so cold I could barely drink it but I did.

It's fully light out now. The air is clear and the sky is blue and the trees are huge and old. The road is rocky and rough and wreaking hell on what's left of the shocks. But I don't care. I'm not going to be returning this car.

I drive up a skinny little gravel road to near the snow line. The trees are thinning out and I can see more sky. It's beautiful, so wide and blue and cold and faraway. I stop the car and roll down all the windows. I stick my head out, like a dog, and it's freezing. I'm giddy with terror, relief and cold. I'm stiff as a doll. I start to shake. I feel like someone is holding me, squeezing me tight and rattling me. I gulp another swig and reach over to the passenger seat for my backpack.

I untie the knot that holds it closed and reach my cold hand in to get what Grandma used to pack: her pistol.

I pull it out and hold it up in both my hands like a blessing or an offering, a sacrifice. It catches sunlight like a jewel, like gold or like a gem. It's glorious! Yet solid, firm inside my hand. It is unmoving. I take it in my right hand and with my left remove from my grubby pockets all my junk: my wallet and change and keys and dirt and lint. I kick off my shoes and peel off my socks and drop them on the floor of the car. I open the door.

The door feels heavy, suddenly. Everything feels solemn, measured, slow. My body feels heavy, ready, grateful.

I stand in the snow. It's very cold. My feet burn and I almost jump, but I withstand. I walk toward the edge of the cliff. I don't look at the footsteps I am leaving.

At the edge of the cliff is a wonderful view. I feel like I can see more than I ever, ever have and it is beautiful.

For a moment it's so beautiful I wonder if I ought to reconsider.

But I know the place is beautiful because of what I'm doing. I feel relief and gratitude because I'm finally doing what I was always meant to. What my whole life has been leading up to. What the dogs were sent to bring me to.

I lift the pistol to my head. I put the end of the barrel to my right temple and press. It feels familiar, like a wedge, a point. My right eye squints. It feels what I've felt before but did not recognize.

I stand there a second and wait although I do not know for what. Am I afraid? Do I regret? Is there another thing I could have done? Or tried? I don't—

It's still and perfectly quiet here. If I could stay here forever, I could, on this clear high white mountain.

But even here, I can't, I can't—

From somewhere, from above? Inside? Behind my head? I hear something. I think it's them.

I look down over the edge of the cliff. Way down there so far I can hardly see, at the end of the air I will hurtle through at the end of my body's life, there is a river.

I press the barrel to my head. I pull the trigger.

24

GARDEN... IN WHICH IS ILLUSTRATED SUCCOR

Something pulled me up beside the river.
Something pulled the dark earth back.

I felt what covered lighten and the dark above was parted.

I was raised.

I felt a mouth against my mouth and something breathed in me and I did too.

Then something moved across my eyes and opened and I saw.

Then something lifted me. I stood.

And then I felt it pull away and I was left alone.

Then I was in the wood and it was dark. The trees around were thick and high. I could not see a sky. But there was light from somewhere though I could not see from where. I walked toward it. I was on a path.

I walked for longer than I thought I could then when I thought that I would fall, I didn't. Then I was at the end of it, and there there was a house.

It was a cottage. A rustic wooden A-frame. Knotted wood. A window on either side of the central front door. Honey colored light coming through the curtains. Smoke curling from the chimney. Pink and blue and yellow flowers in the bed. I followed the stepping stone path to the door and knocked.

I heard no answer. I went inside. The house was clean and warm. There was a table so I sat and there was food and something clean to drink and so I did and there was plenty. There was enough.

I went upstairs and found the bed and slept.

I stayed there in the house alone.

I did not live in idleness. I worked.

Around the house there was a garden and I watered it and tended it. The work was hard and there was nothing else. Neither was there someone else and things that had been once were known. So nothing needed saying and I grew.

Around me all was quiet so I heard what I remembered I had left.

I thought no one had followed me, that I had got away and it was done.

But it was not.

25

CHILD... IN WHICH IS ILLUSTRATED SOLACE

I did not kill the child in the garden. Although it was my burden to uncover her.

I didn't know there was a child or that the child was dead. The dogs made me discover her.

* * *

I lived alone inside the house. The house was far away across the river.

My room upstairs was white and bare. The window in it overlooked the garden. Every day—but never in the night—I worked the garden. I tilled and sowed and planted it. I did the hard work every day but never in the night. The night was always dark.

There was no moon.

Every night before the dark I went upstairs alone. I pulled the curtain closed and I got in my shirt and in the bed and I lay down. I listened to the sounds of night, the settling of earth. I stilled myself.

I never went outside at night. I stayed inside alone. For I was terrified. I lay deep in my cover and I curled around myself and tried to sleep.

But then one night I heard a sound. I woke up to the sound of teeth, the snapping and the claws. I woke up to the sound of awful rutting.

I didn't want to look or see. I lay in bed and curled in tight and hoped that it would go and would not find me.

The next day I went down and saw the damage it had done. I cleaned it up.

It came again that night.

* * *

At first it only stayed a while. It barked and whined and scratched against the trees. When I heard it leave I tried to sleep again.

At first I hoped that it would not come back. Then I hoped eventually it wouldn't, although it always did.

Then there were two. Then three. And when I heard them leave it took me long to fall asleep. Then I hoped eventually they'd finish and would not come back. Every time I told myself it was the last, it had to be.

But then I could not longer hope like that.

Then there were more. Then I told myself that they were not here very long, and I could live through anything a while.

There were only six or eight.

But then there was a pack. A dozen. There were hundreds.

Then I could hear it in their voices, in the digging of their claws. That they were growing bigger. Every fucking one of them was huge.

So I lay in the bed each night and pulled my knees toward my chest and tucked my feet and closed my eyes and put my fists across my eyes and lay so still inside myself I almost didn't breathe. I burrowed in my shirt the way I'd burrow in the earth. I tried to cover up myself but I could always hear them.

Every night I heard them tear the garden. They squeezed in through the hedges and they ripped apart the brush. They split the dark earth open and they pillaged it.

Every night it was the same — no — every night was worse.

Then I began to pray to die. But I could not undo myself.

Then I didn't pray. I only waited.

When they left it was as quiet, almost, as if they'd never been. There was no one else to hear, and no one to believe.

Sometimes I didn't.

But every day when I awoke I picked myself up from the bed and went down to the garden and I saw what they had done. I tried to look away and to forget and I could do that some. But more, I worked. I turned the torn earth over and I made it smooth. I tried to mend what they had torn. Some of it could be revived but some of it was dead.

Every day I did the work.

Every single night they all came back.

I built a fence but they climbed over it.

Upstairs inside the waiting bed I heard them whine and snap. I heard their stomachs scraping where they hadn't cleared the fence. They tore it down.

One night I heard them scratching on the wall outside my room. I bolted to the window and I listened. The sound was terrible so I cried out and suddenly they stopped and the only sound I heard was someone waiting.

I pulled the curtain back and looked and though the night was very dark, it was the blackest night, I saw them.

Their backs were strong and wide and black. Their eager mouths were open and they looked at me. Their muzzles twitched. I heard them grumble low inside their throats. Then one by one and then in groups, they left.

I knew they would come back.

But only once. I knew that having seen me see, the dogs would do me in so I could never tell.

The next day in the garden I did not clean up the wreck. I gathered sticks. I tied the sticks together like a torch. I took an old post from the fence and held it like a club.

That night when the dogs returned, then I went down to them.

My body moved like someone else. I saw my hands pull back the locks and saw my hands take up the club and torch. The light was bronze against the wall. I saw my shadow moving down.

I stood outside and listened. They scraped and dug and panted. I put my hand against the door. The door was smooth and waiting like a skin and I was terrified. I gripped the post and torch. Then I unlocked the door and kicked it open.

I startled them. They stoped their awful rutting and they looked at me. Their eyes were red. I saw the red and black of what they'd torn and I was terrified, I could not move.

But that was only for an instant—though it could have been for years—then I roared it out of me, I leapt down in among them and I shone the light like something fierce and swung the club like something fierce alive.

I swung the club the widest I had ever moved. I felt my arms and shoulders pull, my flexing back and neck. I felt my stomach tighten and my thighs. I felt the air against my skin, the fire in my body. I was opening. I swung the club around so fierce, I slammed the club and lifted it and swung and swung again. I hit and hit and smashed and hit the dogs.

I screamed and yelled and cursed at them. They made these useless little yips but no one heard them. I knocked the stinking breath from them. I beat and smashed their stupid brains and clubbed their bones and guts. I splattered blood and tore their skin and smashed their necks and stomped them down until I couldn't tell, I didn't care, where one of them had ended, where the other was. I kicked their carcasses against, into, each other and I shoved their parts up one another's holes.

I yelled that they deserved it, worse, I yelled at them to not again, no, never, not to anyone. To get the fuck away and not come back.

Then when I had finished, when I got them all and got it out, when everything was almost done, I stopped.

Then everything, almost, was almost quiet. There was no more the sound of them, there only was the sound of something gone.

I closed my eyes. I dropped my face into my hands. My shoulders shook. I tried to hold myself inside. I shook.

I fell to the ground. After a while I kneeled up. I bowed my head and tried to breathe in quietly.

Then something—it was not myself—began to move my hands. My hands were moved along the earth and then were put inside. The hands went down where they had dug. The dogs had almost got what they'd come back for. I put my hands inside the earth, my fingers flexed, I felt me gather up. I dug down in and found what had been buried:

Bones.

I say this was my burden, to uncover her.

The earth down in was wet and dark, like something rich and old but also warm and clean like something good. I removed my shirt and lay it down. I leant above the earth and felt the moon along my naked back. I looked up and I saw the moon where it had never been. My work was lightened.

So I brought up the waiting bones. I brushed the earth from every one and lay it on the shirt. I cleaned each one alone to white, I saw them all alone.

The bones were small and slim and some were broken. Some of them were split or gnawed and some were torn apart.

I went over every one and every piece I took and held as long as it was needed.

I did this through the whole of night, and when the bones were gathered then the night returned to dawn. I smoothed the place the bones had been and tied them in the shirt.

I left the place where I had been and walked down to the river. Though I had never been the way was clear. I walked down to the water's edge. The rising sun was pink then white, the water underneath was white then gold then green with what was growing, then was blue. I held the bones and looked down in the river and I saw myself.

I stepped into the water. It was cold but clean and good, as smooth as oil. I walked out till it came up to my stomach. I held the bones in front of me then lowered them to the surface of the water. I slipped my right hand underneath and with my left untied the shirt. I was careful to lose nothing. I dipped my left hand in the water and I splashed it on the bones. When all the bones were moist I saw them change. They moved a way I recognized.

I saw the body color—pink. The bones were being clothed in flesh, the body was returning to the child.

And when the child was fully formed, I saw what had been done to her: what had been done was the unspeakable. What had been done is what I cannot tell. But I did what I could:

I lay my hands upon the girl and drew out what I could.

I held the child. I poured the water over her and bathed her wounds. The water was smooth as oil and it smelled clean and good.

The neck which had been bruised and stiff returned to white and supple. I washed the scratches off her back. I washed her broken ankles and I held them till they healed. Her fists unclenched inside my palm, her open hands were whole. I wiped my hand across her lips and made them clean. I put my hand across her cheek, it softened under me. I sprinkled water on her face. The child coughed and sputtered and breathed. The child lived again.

Then I annointed both her eyes. She opened them.

She looked at me, inside me still, and so we saw ourselves.

The hands were lifted up and touched the skin. She placed her hand above the place where once had beat my heart. She put our hands above her heart. We felt the beating, two.

She pulled my face toward her face and put her mouth against my ear and told me the unspeakable. I listened and I recognized and told her, Yes, that I believed, and Yes, that I would not forget, and Yes, I told her, Yes, I would remember.

So when what had been buried was unburied, then, and when what was untellable was told, there was release. She put her hands around my face. I bowed my head and closed my eyes and wept.

I wept with the remembering, and what the telling was. I wept with rebecoming, and the bringing back to life of what was dead.

I wept till I was clean. The child held me. And though I longed to stay like that, I knew we must be separate.

So when she loosed her hands from me, I loosed myself from her and stepped away. The water sucked around us and she floated on her back. The white shirt floated underneath her in the water like a sac. She stretched her arms above her head and pulled. Her eyes were closed, the water swept across her face. She rolled onto her stomach and I saw her back. I saw one arm and then the other stroke. Each stroke pulled her away from me and it got hard to see. But every stroke she pulled, the child grew. I saw her light hair darken and her child's limbs grow long. I felt her stomach tighten and her thighs. I saw her body change, I saw the opening.

The river moved toward the light. The light was bright. I held my hands above my eyes until I had to close them from the brilliance. I saw inside what covers me, I see inside the skin:

> *I see the child swimming whole.*
> *I see the water opening.*
> *I see the flesh transported into light.*